Mr.

Claire's heartbeat quickened as she realized he had something to say that was of great import to her. But just as he was about to speak, Lady Sally approached.

"Your mother is coming to take you home, I believe," he said with a heavy sigh.

It seemed to Claire that she and Mr. Bennett would never find a chance to talk alone, and her heart constricted as he took her hand, looked at her slender fingers lying in his own and then released it.

"I shouldn't wonder," he said in a voice totally devoid of emotion, "if Lord Babcock has not sent her to find you. After all, you and he—"

At this point, Mr. Bennett suddenly closed his lips tightly and looked away. Claire tried to search his face for his meaning, tried to divine his thoughts, but it was impossible. Her mother, in a flurry of petticoats, grasped Claire's arm and drew her away.

She failed to notice the dismay on her lovely daughter's face....

THE PARSON'S PLEASURE

PATRICIA WYNN

Harlequin Books

TORONTO • NEW YORK • LONDON
AMSTERDAM • PARIS • SYDNEY • HAMBURG
STOCKHOLM • ATHENS • TOKYO • MILAN

Published April 1988
Second printing June 1988
ISBN 0-373-31022-6

CHAPTER ONE

LADY SALLY burst into the drawing room and found her daughter, the Honourable Miss Claire Oliver, comfortably ensconced in a deep chair reading. "My dear, I have the most interesting news!" she exclaimed. "I have just come from a chance meeting with Lady Sitch who informs me that we are to have a new rector, a Mr. Bennett. That will mean an addition to our dinner parties!"

"Ah! We will be gay to dissipation, now, will we not?" teased Claire, whose experience of the clergy had not led her to expect much from their conversation.

Her irony was not lost on Lady Sally, who laughed and replied, "I did not promise an addition of entertainment to our dinners, but merely of numbers, for it appears that he is a bachelor. So much nicer for us than if he were married, for then we should be obliged to invite his wife, and the two of them would be no addition at all—if you understand me. It was so tedious when our Mr. Twickenham married and we had to support not only his presence but that of his wife. It was too much for your father, an unfair burden, but one couldn't slight them."

"Do you think that Papa will be all that pleased to find a new Mr. Twickenham at his table, married or not?"

"Of course not, my dear, but your father knows his duty, after all. He has promised to call on Mr. Bennett as soon as he is expected to perform that courtesy. And he is well aware of the difficulty in completing a dinner table in our small society. Any newcomer is welcome in some way, especially a single gentleman. He will make a new topic of conversation for those of us who don't get about much. Why, I daresay that Squire Bayless and his good lady have not been more than ten miles from home in the past seven years. Not that your father and I have, either, since he stopped attending the Lords.

"But it will be nice to have someone new, no matter how odious he may turn out to be. If this man is relatively young, and since the living at Garby is a good one, perhaps he will do for your cousin Lydia."

"Oh? And I suppose that Lydia will have nothing to say about it," said Claire in a tone of mock reproach.

"Don't be ridiculous, my dear. You know that the only doubt will be whether Lydia will do for him." And on that practical note, Lady Sally left the room.

Claire was forced to laugh at that uncharitable remark, for her cousin Lydia, though judged a beauty by the standards of the day, had very little to recommend her to the livelier minds in the Oliver family. Lady Sally was quick and gay, with an intelligence that made her slightest utterance a delight to her family. Her high spirits and practical sense made her a good friend, as well as a good parent. Claire's father—Jus-

tin Oliver, fifteenth Baron Oliver—was considerably
older than his wife. He was well-read and studious,
but possessed of a gentle sense of humour which
showed how awake he was to every suit. A somewhat
retiring man, he took much pleasure in the company
of his small family, encouraging the discussion of favourite topics among them. In the absence of a son, he
had come to value the companionship of his daughter, Claire, in a way unusual for the times—as an intellectual equal—and it had been a source of pride for
him to instruct her personally.

She was bright, witty and alive with interest, and
Lord Oliver's efforts had been rewarded with an equal
desire on her part to continue her education as much
as the available supply of books would allow. Besides
her wit, her tendency towards independence and her
robust look of good health made her better fit for an
earlier time, but in the present year of 1819 she was
generally thought to be too tall and slim and healthy-
looking, not to mention bookish, to be fashionable.
No one could fault her gleaming black hair or her
cornflower-blue eyes, but the bloom in her cheeks
suggested a strength of constitution that drew condescending remarks from her Aunt Sophia, Lydia's
mother.

Sophia Willoughby was the wife of the Honourable Robert Willoughby, Lady Sally's younger
brother. Bobby, as he was called by his sister, if not by
his wife, had all of his sister's gaiety and none of her
good sense. He had frittered away his modest inheritance on sport, entertainment and foolish projects,
and had been obliged to rent out his estate for a term,
until he could come about. His brother, the Earl of

Dillingham, had tired of Robert's many vicissitudes
and was not disposed to help him again. So it had been
arranged for the Willoughbys to let a cottage on Lord
Oliver's property until their fortune should be restored, but as Robert's sense had not noticeably improved since his coming, no one expected a speedy
return to the prior status.

The proximity of the Willoughbys had naturally led
them to an assumption of intimacy, which the Oliver
family would have preferred to live without, particularly because of the difference in temperaments between the female members of the families. Still, the
Olivers were determined to carry out their family responsibilities as best they could.

And indeed, Lady Sally and Claire truly pitied Lydia, for it was not expected that that young woman
would have much of a dowry when Robert had been
so wasteful. Consequently, making a successful match
for her daughter had become the urgent occupation of
Mrs. Willoughby to the exclusion of all else. In this she
was fully justified, for the only alternatives open to
Lydia, failing matrimony, were to become a govern-
ess or a companion to a relative or some elderly person of fortune—all dismal prospects. The best that
could be hoped for her realistically was marriage to a
younger son, someone who, having inherited no
property, had had to find a living in the Church or the
military.

Claire, on the other hand, had a fortune settled
upon her of thirty thousand pounds, which had attracted many a prospective husband during her one
season in London. However, this competence had allowed her to be more critical of the men who pre-

sented themselves, and her London season had been a disappointment. Accustomed as she was to the easy camaraderie of her parents and their full trust in her judgement, she found that the men she had met in town expected much less of her intellectually and emotionally. The amusements that her mother had described from memories of her own London season, which had stirred much excitement in Claire, were all there, but dismayingly different for many reasons.

The gayness and frivolity had a forced quality which had not existed even so recently as before Waterloo. The soldiers who had taken part in the recent hostilities had come home to find hard times and a Regent who continued, despite all, to spend sums beyond their imaginations on pure pleasure. The year before had seen riots all over London, and in the January of Claire's London season, the Regent had been pelted with stones on his way to open Parliament. Some said he had even been fired upon. Yet that same month he hosted at the Brighton Pavilion a dinner party at which his French chef, Carême, served thirty-six entrées. Though the aristocracy continued to amuse themselves, it was with the French Revolution fresh in their minds, and many lived in expectation of seeing the mob at their doors.

The London of Claire's season sadly missed the personalities of recent years. Beau Brummell had left England to escape arrest for debts, taking with him his attractive impudence. And Lord Byron, the Romantic hero, had been forced to choose exile over social ostracism as rumours of his outrageous love life spread. Shock and revulsion had swept society, resulting in a moralizing temper.

Claire's upbringing had not prepared her for the shifting moods of the current society. Women had begun a retreat into ignorance, coyness and oblivion, encouraged by the men into all sorts of affectation. Frequently Claire wished that she could have given her chance at a London season to Lydia, who had been schooled in all the requisite manners and who would have valued the opportunity more than she. And she would have offered it to her, but she knew that Lydia's dowry was so small that even a London season would not have brought her a proper offer.

To spare her own parents disappointment, Claire had never let them know that her season had not been ideal. It led her, however, to muse upon the steps she should take regarding her own future now that, at twenty-two, marriage no longer appeared to be likely.

She was interrupted in her reverie by the sound of voices in the hall and the subsequent entry of her Aunt Sophia and Lydia into the drawing room. Their cottage being but a mile away, they came on foot for their frequent calls, though their apparent exertion suggested a much longer trip. They both sat down gingerly on the edges of their chairs.

"Claire, dear," began her aunt, "I must beg of you some refreshment, though more for Lydia than for myself, for she is much too delicate for that walk. I declare, if only Mr. Willoughby could afford to keep a carriage, we should never venture to visit you in this manner."

"Indeed," said Claire, "you should not put yourself to the trouble so frequently if it discomforts you." But she hurried to ask the footman to bring some cool drinks because Lydia did look uncomfortably flushed due, Claire suspected, more to her tight stays than to the delicacy of her constitution or the length of the walk. On returning to the drawing room, she tactlessly remarked upon the colour in her cousin's cheeks, which drew a worried look from her aunt.

"You must be mistaken, child, for I see no evidence of colour. Perhaps just a shade, but you know how hot these afternoons are. I am sure that it will pass as soon as we have regained our composure, for you know that few young ladies can boast so fair a complexion as my Lydia."

Lydia, who was only slightly less ruffled than her mother by the offence, said, "Thank you for your concern, cousin, but my mother's attentions to my complexion are such that you need have no fear for it. Indeed she is very particular in her treatments and insists that I drink a certain amount of strong vinegar and take chalk occasionally—though not at the same time as the vinegar, for that is most uncomfortable."

Mrs. Willoughby looked proudly at her daughter, then turned to Claire. "I recommend these methods to you, Niece, since they come from the highest authority on female beauty. They were described in *The Ladies' Magazine* by Dr. Barnes, a well-respected physician, and he assures that there is no harm in them."

"I am always grateful for your suggestions, my dear aunt, but I meant no disparagement of Lydia's complexion. Indeed, she has a fairness of which I am certain you must be proud. I meant only to comment that perhaps the heat had been too much for her. But I see that she is quite recovered and the flush is gone."

This speech much gratified her aunt who resumed her normal look of complacency, but it was really intended to turn the conversation away from one of her most favoured topics, which was to discuss why Claire had returned from London two years before without an engagement, in spite of her fortune. As far as Sophia was concerned, the only reason could be Claire's inattention to the cultivation of ladylike qualities, such as a languid pallor, an air of helplessness and a waist nipped in by corseting until all voluntary movement was curtailed, to name but a few. Claire believed in mild exercise for ladies and used no hard stays in her corset, though the gradual return of the waistline to its proper position, now almost complete, had brought them back into style. She considered herself fortunate that a natural slimness permitted her to enjoy greater freedom of movement than her cousin did with her tight corseting.

Her aunt deplored Claire's habits, as well as her refusal to wear even the smallest padding of the bosom, which could be skilfully used to hide her imperfections from the male eye. Lydia, short—her mother would say "diminutive"—and plump, needed only tight lacing to be the picture of fashion. Sophia envied Claire her money and position, for had Lydia been blessed with the same fortuitous situation, she would have been dressed to perfection and introduced properly into society.

Lady Sally returned from outdoors, where she had been cutting roses for the drawing room. "Good afternoon, Sophia, Lydia. I suppose you have heard the news."

"What news is that, Sally?" questioned Sophia with interest, as there was not often anything new to report in the neighbourhood.

"Why, that there is to be a new rector for Garby parish. Lady Sitch informed me of his expected arrival just this morning, though I have not heard much more. His name is Bennett and I know that he was at Oxford. She did not have time to say more."

"Is there a Mrs. Bennett?" asked Sophia, going right to the essentials.

"No, isn't it fortunate? Not that I want the poor man to be lonely, but it is always so pleasant to speculate upon the appearance and the qualities of a single man before one meets him," said Lady Sally mischievously.

Claire decided not to add that one was almost inevitably disappointed, considering the plans her mother had in mind for the new Mr. Bennett.

Mrs. Willoughby frowned slightly and stiffened, but merely because she considered this to be a frivolous treatment of the clergy, whom she held in the greatest respect and thought above all speculation. "I will encourage Mr. Willoughby to call upon him as soon as possible, for I am sure that he will want to cultivate the association. I always say that there is nothing so inspiring to proper behaviour as frequent association with men of the cloth. They must be and are a continual source of enlightenment to those of us who are not in that state of grace which they command."

Lady Sally, who did not in the least believe that her brother would welcome the association, hastened to agree and to change the subject, knowing that her sister-in-law's only enjoyment in her marriage, and perhaps her reason for marrying, had been the romantic notion of improving her husband. She intended to be his conscience and his inspiration, and indeed was the only evidence of either in Bobby.

The conversation took a more general turn until Mrs. Willoughby noticed the book her niece had put down.

"What is that you were reading, Claire?"

"It is merely a treatise on the principles of morals in legislation," she replied, readying herself for battle, "written by Mr. Jeremy Bentham."

Her aunt was shocked.

"Sally, I wonder that you should consider that an appropriate study for a young lady," attacked her aunt, pleading to what she thought of as a mother's finer feelings.

"My husband found Mr. Bentham's writing to make comfortable reading, Sophia, so I do not think you need fear for Claire. It is not likely to lead to brain fever. Besides, Claire is a woman now and must be trusted to use her own judgement about what to read."

"At times I think you are far too liberal a parent, Sally, though I am sure you mean well. I am still not convinced that such reading is not harmful." An alarming thought occurred to her and she turned to Claire. "You are not reading that after consuming a large meal?" she exclaimed.

Claire assured her that she had only lightly partaken of luncheon, immediately seeing the association in her aunt's mind. Serious mental exercise was thought to be dangerous after a heavy meal.

Sophia, somewhat mollified, continued, "I might suggest to you, Sally, some other occupations for

Claire, which are thought to be perfect ones for a young lady; conchology, for example, is unexceptionable. Lydia enjoys it so. Some of the objects that she is adorning with shells are quite attractive: covered boxes, reticules, even lamps!''

Claire, who thought no occupation more uninspiring than attaching little shells to everything, felt a cloud of depression settle upon her. She knew perfectly well that her mother would ridicule the idea as much as she, but it was somehow lowering to feel that the rest of the world, as exemplified by her aunt, expected her to spend her time in such a way.

Sophia, seeing the unacceptance in Claire's face, tried to interest her in improving her needlework. But Lady Sally deftly managed to turn the conversation again to Lydia, who had been sitting, as usual, in dutiful silence while her mother pontificated, and Claire was once more saved the need to reply. She had noticed during the past year that her aunt was taking more of an interest in her welfare, did indeed seem quite concerned about her. She must think her a hopeless case, destined to be an old maid.

Lydia as a topic of conversation soon being exhausted, the ladies fell back on the most consuming topic the county had enjoyed for many years—the extensive remodelling of Lord Sitch's estate. The Earl of Sitch, having come into large amounts of new money when coal was discovered under his property in Wales, had undertaken a modernization of his once charming manor. The result was unrecognizable. Not only was the present house three times the size of the former, but it also had taken on the appearance of a medieval castle, complete with battlements adorning the front. The work had been going on for two years and was nearing completion.

"I suppose we will soon be receiving cards for a great unveiling, a ball or some such," said Lady Sally. "Really, it will be quite exciting to see the changes."

"Yes, the moat will be completed soon. Lady Sitch informed me that it is the last major improvement before the garden is laid out," contributed her sister-in-law.

"The moat?" questioned Lady Sally and Claire in unison, disbelief in their tones.

"Yes, of course the moat," asserted Sophia defensively. "At least, a partial moat. The architect added it after the original plans were made, I understand. A charming idea, in my opinion."

Lady Sally could not let this pass. "I fail to see the necessity for a moat in this day and age, Sophia. Surely Lord Sitch does not expect some baron, such as my husband, to rise up and lay siege to his household."

At this, Lydia and her mother laughed affectionately. "Nonsense, my dear sister! The moat is purely decorative. It does not even completely encircle the castle. The whole spirit of the improvement is one of the Gothic period. The addition of the great hall will show this, I believe. The effect will be reminiscent of one's noblest ancestors."

Lady Sally looked at her and exclaimed in shocked tones, "The Goths! Surely not, Sophia!"

Claire had to turn away to smother a smile. Lydia looked confused. And Sophia, momentarily disconcerted, recovered with an air of briskness.

"Don't be silly, Sally. Of course, I do not mean the Goths. I was speaking of our ancestors to whom we owe the building of our great cathedrals."

Claire's face told her mother that what Sophia Willoughby knew about any of those people could be stated in one sentence. Of the nobility of the earl's ancestors, too, she had doubts, since the title had originated only in the past century. However, that small problem had been addressed. Lord Sitch, who was on the fringe of the Carlton House set, was to be honoured by his "dear friend" the Prince Regent with a new family name—Sitchville—which, it was hoped, would give the impression that his ancestors came over with the Conqueror.

"The moat," Sophia continued, "will be seen from all the public rooms along the front of the house. To cross it, one must use an adorable little drawbridge, which does not rise, however. I am merely repeating what dear Lady Sitch—or should I say Sitchville—was kind enough to describe to me," Sophia concluded, reading disbelief in her listeners' faces.

"I am certain you are right, Sophia," Lady Sally assured her, taking pity. "It is just that I am sadly out of fashion, it seems. I fail to see the need for such changes. I confess I was rather attached to the old manor house. It held many pleasant memories for me; I remember attending balls there since I was a girl. Indeed, it was there I met your father, Claire."

"We must not stand in the way of progress, Sally," said her sister-in-law with a condescending smile on her face, for she did consider her in-laws to be dismally old-fashioned in their views.

"No, indeed, that would never do," added Lady Sally in her most pleasant, if insincere, voice. "My chief interests in the entire project, I confess, will be the servants' quarters and the conveniences, which I expect will be truly magnificent and up-to-date, and therefore most instructive. In that respect, I think Lord Sitch will have done something to benefit all of us who live retired in the country. We have no other opportunity to learn about the improvements modern science has achieved, but Lord Sitch's frequent trips to London will have educated him in these matters."

In this, Mrs. Willoughby could not acquiesce quickly enough, as she always did when the Sitch-villes were praised. And her respect for them was genuine, since in addition to their position in society, which she naturally respected, they appeared to believe in and uphold all the most up-to-date social values. Lady Sitchville and she were true soulmates, she was certain, and only the disparity in their fortunes kept them from being the closest of friends.

Presently the Willoughby ladies rose to go, and with an air of speeding the parting guests Lady Sally preceded them to the door. To Claire's consternation, her aunt held back as if to have a private word with her. She took a piece of paper out of her reticule, and with modestly lowered eyes and a real blush on her cheeks, held it out to Claire.

"Niece, I know you will forgive me for touching on this most personal subject," she said hesitantly, obviously in acute embarrassment, "for you know that my concern for you is constant and of the most affectionate kind. This is a little secret that I think might be of benefit to you. It was confided to me many years ago by someone in whom I have the utmost confidence. I have been most assiduous in encouraging Lydia with her applications, with you see what result, though this must be between us." She raised her eyes briefly to Claire's bemused face, touched the hand that now held the paper and said, "Do not thank me, my dear. There will be no need to mention it again." With this, she nearly fled from the room.

With a sense of dread, Claire opened the paper and read. Her worst suspicions were confirmed when she saw what was enclosed.

The following preparation, very softly rubbed upon the bosom for five or ten minutes, two or three times a day, will promote its growth.

Tincture of Myrrh	½ oz.
Pimpernel Water	4 oz.
Elder-Flower Water	4 oz.
Musk	1 gr.
Rectified Spirit of Wine	6 oz.

Intense colour infused Claire's face, but not from embarrassment. When Lady Sally returned to the parlour, she was surprised to find her daughter pacing the floor at an alarmingly unladylike speed. Her hands were pressed to her cheeks and she was making a noise like a steam whistle.

"My love, what is the matter?" Lady Sally cried.

Claire thrust the paper at her and continued her pacing. "Really, Mother," she replied at last, "she has gone too far this time. I have had quite enough of her...concern." Claire drawled this last word.

Lady Sally quickly scanned the sheet of paper, then collapsed in giggles into an armchair. When she was able to control herself to a reasonable degree, she confronted her daughter's daggerlike glare.

"My poor precious dear," she said lovingly. "You must not let her get to you this way. The really ridiculous thing about it all is that she does mean to be of help to you. She honestly thinks these matters are of as much concern to you as they are to herself, and by all reckoning they must be thought to consume her!"

"But it is all so insulting! Chalk for my face! Lemon juice and vinegar for my hands! Deer fat on my limbs! Now this! Why doesn't she just tell me I look like a cow and have done with it?"

"Because you don't look like a cow, you silly girl. She doesn't realize that you find this insulting, because she knows you to be a very attractive young woman. She just enjoys talking about these things to the exclusion of much else. Also, as we both are unfortunately aware, every ladies' magazine for the past many years has been full of just such nonsense, and short, plump figures such as Lydia's are just the thing. The Willoughby women don't have much to boast about, so let them have this one small matter for pride. If you ask me, though, I would have to say that I don't think men care tuppence for half the things the magazines say they do. And imagine some young man's surprise on his wedding night to find that half of what he thought was his fiancée is only so much padding!"

Claire had to laugh. "Excellent! I must point that out to Aunt Sophia."

"You wicked girl! You will do nothing of the kind," shrieked Lady Sally. "She would be horrified to think

I spoke to you of such a thing. You must never give me away or we shall have no peace around here." Then, seeing that she had restored her daughter to her customary good humour, she went off to confer with the cook about menus, leaving Claire to her thoughts.

CHAPTER TWO

NOT ALL OF HER THOUGHTS were happy, however, for Claire could not help but be disturbed about her future. Perhaps it was silly to despair of ever meeting an acceptable gentleman to marry when one was only twenty-two, but the neighbourhood was too small to present newcomers except on the rarest of occasions. Besides, Claire thought, if she had not been happy with any of the numerous male acquaintances she had made in London, how could she expect to be pleased with someone she might meet at a local assembly or ball, few as there were? Nor was she unmindful of her position in society, which, coming from good family and large fortune, limited her to persons of equal rank. Fully aware of the unusual and, to her, ideal nature of her parents' marriage, she could not be content to accept less. Her aunt's marriage, for example, was of a sort which was unacceptable to her. Much as she was fond of her uncle, Claire could perceive that nothing would be worse than to be married to such an irresponsible person.

No, marriage was not for her. So what was it to be, then? She had frequently thought that if she had been a man, she would have loved to make the Grand Tour. She could perhaps have found employ in the Orient in one of the trading companies; but of course employment would not have been necessary, because as a man she would have been her father's heir. As it was now, her family's estate was entailed upon the nearest male relative, in this instance a distant cousin, so someday in the future it was understood that Claire would have to remove herself from her home. It was a sad thought, but she knew that she was much more fortunate than others who had no fortune to secure their futures.

Claire had been formulating a vague plan in her mind ever since she had returned from London. It had begun with a wish that she might find a future for herself that would not depend upon some other person. Though ill-defined, her wish had now become an idea with merely the details to be worked out, but she felt she had a good deal of time to worry about them. She intended, upon her father's death, to remove to Bath with her mother—if she, and most likely she would be, given the more than twenty years difference in ages between her husband and her, were still living—and to let a small house in an agreeable part of town.

In spite of the disappointment Claire had experienced in London, she knew that a city would have a great number of pleasures to offer to compensate them somehow for the loss of her father's company. With their finances entrusted to a well-chosen firm of solicitors, she and her mother should be able to live quite comfortably. She doubted that they would go out much in society, but there would be the libraries, the baths and the theatre to amuse them. Claire smiled to think that they would be labelled eccentrics, but suspected that neither she nor her mother would care. It was an unusual plan, but as far as she could tell, she and her family were unusual.

Claire had never confided this plan to her parents and had no intention of broaching the subject until they expressed a concern for her future. They would be happy to see her comfortably settled, but they were not really eager to lose her and were not anxious for her to leave home soon. She knew that the time would come when they would realize that she was getting a little old for marriage and would begin to ask questions. Until then, she would keep her own counsel and enjoy life with them as it was.

She had a serious turn of mind in some areas in which young ladies were not supposed to have an interest. Other matters that were considered to be proper ones for ladies only tickled her sense of the ridiculous. She had a thorough understanding of the moralizing mood of the day without being taken in by its hypocrisy. Claire thought at times that she should try her hand at becoming a novelist, for in spite of her serious nature, she was not above enjoying a good novel. Her favourite writer was Jane Austen, but she had vastly enjoyed the Gothic tales of Mrs. Radcliffe, from her mother's generation, and the recent *Frankenstein*, by the poet Shelley's wife, Mary. Reading these, she had often thought of trying her hand, and she thought that she could make a heroine swoon quite as well as did Mrs. Kitty Cuthbertson.

Her Aunt Sophia was addicted to the works of the Evangelicals, both the penny tracts and the "improving" novels. She thought them instructional to young girls, for they taught proper subordination to author- and checked inquisitive tendencies in young minds.

Just that week, Mrs. Willoughby had tried to press upon Claire a novel in which the heroine refused her love's quite honourable offer of marriage and eternal happiness because her parents did not wish it. What annoyed Claire the most about the tale was the author's suggestion that this daughterly virtue yielded the young heroine a more satisfying happiness than would have marriage to the man of her dreams.

Others of her aunt's favourites held up for praise were stories of young ladies who appeared to have no other occupation than prayer and constant attendance upon a dying parent. Such conduct, Claire trusted, would drive her own parents mad.

The most unpalatable of these stories were those which portrayed the grim harvest of young ladies who gave in to the temptations of sin. They were invariably disowned by their families and left out in the elements to die, even though in Claire's limited experience quite the opposite occurred. There was scandal attached to these things, of course, but the families of the young ladies usually took an active role in settling their wayward offspring as comfortably as possible, arranging marriages if they could.

Sophia would have been shocked to know that Claire was reasonably well-informed on these matters, for she carefully shielded Lydia from all the more sordid facts of life even when presented in their most objective form. She was careful, however, to instruct her as to their horrors, all the while cloaking them in such a mystery that they became the object of much mistaken conjecture and avid curiosity. Lady Sally took a far more practical view of her daughter's education, and from an early date had spoken quite openly about the undeniable aspects of human nature. As a result Claire was able to face life more calmly than poor Lydia, since her fear of the unknown was lessened.

As her thoughts turned to Lydia, Claire heard a soft creaking of the floorboards outside the drawing room which usually signalled the presence of her cousin's other parent. And indeed, when the door was cracked open, Robert Willoughby's face peeked around the corner. On seeing Claire, he whispered conspiratorially, "Has your aunt left?" When Claire gave him the all-clear he straightened and entered more boldly.

He lowered himself as slowly into a chair as his portliness would allow and looked at his niece with a self-satisfied expression on his face. This Claire interpreted as pleasure at once again having successfully evaded his wife on the way in. From behind a rather heavy mop of hair and side whiskers, his face beamed out with a red glow which she attributed partly to a lifetime of frequent overdrink and partly to a long walk on an unseasonably warm day. There was a glint in his eye, much the same as that in a puppy who has slipped its leash to prance just out of reach.

"What *have* you been up to, Uncle Bobby?" Claire asked affectionately.

"Up to?" blurted Robert with a guilty start. "Why, nothing, nothing. Sorry to have missed her, that's all."

Claire decided not to respond to this patent lie, but raised her eyes heavenwards as if to remind him of another listener.

"Now don't go lookin' like your aunt, girl. It don't become you," he scolded. Then realizing that he had again said something he shouldn't have, he continued rapidly, "Been up to see Sitch's new colt, Sarravano. Now that's a fine one. Got a new man as trainer, too. Says he's going to enter him in the Derby, and what's more, he claims he'll win it! I call that poor!"

"Whatever do you mean, Uncle?" Claire asked, amused.

"It's unfair!" he exclaimed. "What does a rich man like Sitch need with a Derby winner? He's got more than he deserves or needs already, if you ask me. Why, the man's got so many horses the place looks like Tattersall's!"

"Lord Sitch has every right to own those horses," Claire stated calmly, painfully aware of her uncle's style of logic. "He buys them with the income from his estates which, since he appears to be good at husbandry, he has earned by his own hard work."

"Well, don't you see? That's just the point!" he blustered. "What's he need to work for when he has all that soft? I call it greedy!"

Claire tried to control her exasperation as she attempted to explain to her uncle that Lord Sitchville's wealth was in part the result of his efforts, but she realized that it was a connection which Uncle Bobby was unable to make. At times it worried her that his twisted reasoning bordered on the amoral, though part of his charm was his illogic. It occurred to her to wonder whether it wasn't all an act on his part, prompted by laziness. As he was generally thought to be irresponsible and something of a character, no one ever expected anything of him and he was free to spend all his time pleasing himself. Of course, Mrs. Willoughby tried to improve him, but Uncle Bobby

continued to be a rogue, changing only in the degree
to which he voiced his nonsensical outlook on things.

"I had a good chat with that trainer of his," he said,
returning to the subject on his mind. "Not a bad fellow. Name's Tucker. Knows a thing or two about
horses, too. He says that Sarravano will finish way
ahead of his field. I asked him about Sir George
Frederick's colt, Magnifico, and he says that one's
Sarravano's only rival. Could be a close race, I said,
but Tucker says no, Sitch's colt's the best. Anyway,"
he added, "Tucker's probably right. Seems he's been
employed as trainer in a number of the finest stables."

"If that is so," questioned Claire, unconsciously
trying to dampen his enthusiasm since she well knew
his gullibility, "then why has he chosen to come this
far into the country to Lord Sitch's—Lord Sitchville's—service?" With an effort, she used the new
name.

But Robert brushed her query aside impatiently.
"Why shouldn't he? He knows a good thing when he
sees one. Sitch's paying him a pretty penny, let me tell
you! A man with his experience don't come cheap.
Yessir, he could tell you a thing or two about horses,
my girl, and about the Derby, so don't look so suspi-
cious."

Something about this speech made Claire think that
it was almost word for word what the trainer had told
her uncle about himself, but she refrained from commenting. She knew that her Aunt Sophia would not
encourage Robert to spend his time around Lord
Sitchville's stables, developing a friendship with this
Tucker. His interest in horses had already been re-

sponsible in large part for their misfortune, and he was easily taken in by boasters when they touched upon his favourite subject.

Claire was suddenly reminded of her earlier conversation with her aunt, and she could not resist the opportunity to tease her uncle. She turned to him with a twinkle in her eye.

"You will be interested to know, Uncle Bobby, that there is to be a new rector at Garby. Aunt Sophia was just telling us that she is certain you will be anxious to pay him a call as soon as possible."

Robert glared at her so much like a pouting schoolboy, despite his bushy eyebrows, that Claire had to laugh out loud.

"You may laugh, my girl, but I do not see the humour in it! How would you like it, eh? When I think of the number of times she made me call on that old windbag Twickenham, my blood boils. And what good did it do, I ask you? Just so he could prose on and on about the Scriptures—as if I didn't have enough of that from your aunt. A man can't get any peace in his own home these days!"

Claire, not realizing what a hornets' nest she would stir up, hastened to soothe his temper. "I understand that Mr. Bennett is a younger man than Mr. Twickenham, so perhaps he will be easier to converse with."

"No, they're all alike," replied Bobby, though he looked somewhat relieved at the news. "Still, if he's a younger one, he might be a little more humble—something they could all use, a little humility."

"Now then, Uncle Bobby, you know perfectly well that nothing could exceed the humility of Mr. Twickenham. Why, I am sure that Papa frequently wished he would speak up a little more for himself."

"Don't let that fool you, niece. That was the face he put on for your father. That old hypocrite knew where his bread was buttered. He also knew that he would never get a farthing out of me, no matter what Sophia wanted. Oh, he knew how to ingratiate himself with her, all right, but he wanted nothing to do with the likes of me. The feeling was mutual, too."

Though Claire had never observed the old rector display such behaviour, she felt that her uncle's revelations had a certain ring of truth. It could never have been a pleasure, nor even have done much good, for Mr. Twickenham to speak to her uncle, who was entirely unreceptive to such counsel. But in justice to her uncle she had to admit that they had long suspected the former rector of less than pure motives in his attention to the Oliver family. Lord Oliver had no livings at his disposal, but he was rich and well connected, and that was enough to recommend him to a dependent clergyman with some ambition.

"No, I didn't have much use for old Twickenham," Bobby continued, "though he let loose with a good story or two when he had enough port under his belt. You know why I called on him the way I did?" he asked. "It wasn't to please Sophia, oh, no. It was because it tickled me to keep him away from his fishing." He laughed at the remembrance.

Now in a lighter mood, Bobby decided the moment was right to tease his niece. "They say that Babcock is coming back from London for good," he said, with such a suggestive tone in his voice that Claire looked startled, turned to him and blushed with annoyance.

Cecil Sitchville, Viscount Babcock, was Lord Sitchville's eldest son and heir. Slightly older than Claire, he was an unimaginative young man who, because of his responsible position, had decided that it was his duty to marry a lady of the county. It followed logically, therefore, that Claire, who had the highest standing of any single lady in the area, should be favoured with his choice. Since he calmly and arrogantly assumed that his suit would be welcomed by anyone, he had persistently comported himself as though the engagement were a *fait accompli* whenever he returned home, this in spite of the fact that he received no encouragement from either Claire or her parents. He seemed to assume that he had only to speak and his bachelorhood would end, and he was waiting until the day he should desire this to be so.

More than once Claire had had occasion to be glad of her independent means, a circumstance which would allow her to give a resounding "No" when that most unpleasant day should arrive. Meanwhile, whenever Babcock was in the county, his steady attentions were embarrassing and ever a source of irritation. Claire's uncle was dimly aware of this, although he wondered whether her irritation was due to the fact that the viscount had not yet spoken. Her blush of annoyance now convinced him that there existed some reason for discomfort.

When Claire did not answer, Robert proceeded with his teasing. "They say he will be coming home to learn the estate business in preparation for taking over the management of part of Sitch's properties. If that's the case he ought to be marrying soon. Quite a matrimonial prize, that one. Heir to the largest fortune in the county, not to mention all those horses. Wonder who he'll expect to stand up with him?''

Claire was grateful for the sudden entry of her mother into the room, which put an end to Robert's speculation and spared her from having to answer, for Uncle Bobby would not tease her in her mother's presence. Claire found it annoying that even her own uncle should be under a misconception about her relationship with Lord Babcock. She knew that he would not be able to understand her complete lack of interest in the young man, so she had no intention of discussing it with him. But she admitted to herself that it would be a rare person who could understand her complete indifference toward such a matrimonial prize, and she had enough sense to realize that the Willoughbys, in their dependent state, would be the last to do so. For at least the hundredth time, Claire thanked her stars for her financial independence. She would rather be plagued by fortune-hunters than in need of accepting the first offer to come round.

CHAPTER THREE

IN DUE COURSE, Lord Oliver made his call upon Mr.
Bennett and extended an invitation to dine the following week. But, amused by his ladies' curiosity, he
had not been very forthcoming with answers to their
many questions about the new rector. In reply to
queries about his appearance, he merely said that he
was neither quite so short nor quite so pear-shaped as
Mr. Twickenham. And since Mr. Twickenham had
been very short and pear-shaped indeed, this left much
room for conjecture. The ladies settled between them
that the new rector was of medium height and of slight
build, with perhaps a gentle bulge in the middle, since
any clergy of their acquaintance had shown the bene-
fits of dining often at others' tables. They were di-
vided over his dress, Lady Sally imagining a barely
suppressed dandyism and Claire expecting a puritan
severity such as that affected by Twickenham. The
baron enjoyed this speculation and laughed heartily at
their attempts to get his confirmation, but he refused
to give anything away. He did allow that his call had
been unusually entertaining and enlightening, but
would not elaborate, leaving mother and daughter to
suspect that there was something more than a little
amusing about Mr. Bennett.

The week passed without any of their questions being answered, for the Willoughbys, a possible source of information, had yet to meet the rector, Mr. Willoughby having not performed his social duties toward the new reverend. Thus it was that when their dinner guest was announced, Claire was stunned to see a tall, athletically built man enter the room. As he moved closer, she perceived that he was not only tall, he was the tallest man she had ever met! He was simply but elegantly dressed in fawn-coloured trousers and a dark tailcoat with velvet lapels, which was unbuttoned according to custom. His waistcoat was silk, dark like his coat, his cravat white. The tips of his collar were worn at a modest height, and the tying of his cravat showed that neither too little nor too much attention had been given to it. His bearing and his style had a hint of the military, which drew attention to the expanse of strong chest, an expanse which would have been plainly evident without them.

His face was distinctive rather than handsome, with lines that attested to both humour and sensitivity, but there was a trace of some care, some worry, consciously hidden. His hair was cut short, and curled naturally. From this first meeting, Claire had the overall impression of a pleasant personality; but there was something more she could not interpret. Then she realized to her surprise that the politeness in his countenance was designed to conceal the anticipation of an evening spent in boredom! Lord Oliver greeted his guest and then turned to present Mr. Christopher Bennett to his family. When the rector took the hand she offered him, Claire lowered her eyelashes and blushed to think of the meek, languid Mr. Bennett of

their imaginings. Mr. Bennett was not totally blind to
the reason for this confusion, since the surprise that
greeted his six feet, four inches on most first meetings
was frequently followed by embarrassment. In spite of
his accustomedness to this kind of reception, he did
notice that a blush became Miss Oliver very well. He
had caught a glimpse of deep blue eyes before they
fell, and silently complimented her on her choice of
dress, a fine white lawn gown cut straight across the
breast with pink embroidery, the colour of which
seemed to match the bloom in her cheeks. As for
Claire, she thought she must be becoming quite provincial indeed if meeting a clergyman, however different from her expectations, could throw her into
such a flutter.

Following the instructions, general conversation
was exchanged about the weather and the difficulties
Mr. Bennett had encountered—or not encountered—
in finding the Oliver property, until dinner was announced. All the while, Lady Sally could not keep her
gaze from wandering to the top of Mr. Bennett's head
as she compared his size to the familiar things in her
drawing room and speculated upon his exact height.
At first Mr. Bennett was inclined to think that there
was something peculiar about his hair, but being of a
quick mind, he guessed what she was about. So when
he offered her his arm to take her in to dinner, he bent
his head and whispered obligingly, "That would be
six-foot-four, Lady Sally."

Lady Sally gasped and blushed upon being found
out, but after turning and seeing the smile on his face,
she rapped his hand with her fan. As she told her husband later, she had not felt so young in years. "You

have no right to be so saucy," she whispered back to him. "You know very well that it is quite improper in a clergyman."

Mr. Bennett only chuckled by way of reply.

After he had led her to her seat and was making his way to his own, Lady Sally managed to whisper to Claire, "He *is* quite handsome; it is too bad that he is to be wasted on Lydia."

Claire glanced at the rector in time to see a cocked eyebrow and a twitch at his lips, and she suspected that he had caught her mother's words. As he seated himself opposite Claire, he looked up and caught her watching him. The frank amusement in his expression put her out of countenance and she busied herself with her napkin until Lord Oliver began to speak.

"Bennett," he said, and then paused. "That is Avonley's name, I believe."

Mr. Bennett acknowledged the statement with reserve. "My cousin John is the eighth earl. My father was his uncle."

Lord Oliver darted a look at Lady Sally who was making an effort to conceal the consternation this response had aroused in her. Then he renewed the conversation.

"Would your father have been the Honourable Sylvester Bennett?"

Mr. Bennett nodded.

"I never knew him," said Lord Oliver. "He was somewhat older than I, but I remember hearing quite well of him. An experimenter, was he not?"

Mr. Bennett seemed to warm to the praise of his father. He smiled and replied, "He was interested in everything and tried his hand at it all—mechanical devices, science, architecture—a host of other subjects. Some of his plant studies are still considered to be definitive."

"You seem quite young to be his son," observed Lord Oliver.

"Yes, I believe I was quite a surprise to both my parents, but they held up under it quite well." He smiled gently. "Unfortunately, they have both been gone these fifteen years."

"Your cousin I have met from time to time at Lord Sitch's residence. They are on quite good terms," said Lord Oliver without any particular emphasis.

The rector resumed an air of reserve and replied, "They are bosom companions, in fact. You perceive that I owe my present position to my cousin's influence. I was made his ward upon my parents' death." This was said with a stiffness and lack of expression that belied the gratitude in his words. He did not elaborate, nor seem to wish to discuss his family further, so they conversed briefly about his educational background. Lord Oliver found many similarities in their experiences to discuss, and warming to his guest, he began to take an interest in his opinions.

"Are you acquainted with Mr. Copley, Lord Sitch's man in Parliament?" asked the baron, refusing to cater to Lord Sitchville's vanity by using the new name.

"One has heard of him, naturally," replied Mr. Bennett with an evident lack of enthusiasm, which Lord Oliver noted with approval. Mr. Copley was not a favourite of his, for the man had been quite outspoken in support of repressive measures after the attack on the Regent.

"It is my understanding that Lord Sitch...ville," the rector continued with a strange emphasis, "has more than four boroughs in his gift."

He was referring, Claire knew, to the electoral system of the time in which the vote was given solely to landowners. There being few of these in some areas, the power to send a member to Parliament could rest with only a handful of men, or a single man.

"Yes," Lord Oliver answered dryly, "and two of them are little more than cow pastures."

"Would there be Jersey or Guernsey cows in those pastures, Papa?" inquired Claire seriously, but with a twinkle in her eye.

"I am not sure, my dear." He turned to her with a smile. "Why do you ask? Is it pertinent to our discussion?"

"That remains to be seen," she said, glancing again at their guest. "I am conducting a study to determine whether Jersey or Guernsey cows are more likely to return a Tory member to Parliament."

"And what will you do with this information?" her father asked, amusement lighting his face.

"Why, encourage the propagation of the other breed, of course," she stated firmly, not fearing to show her true political leanings.

"My dear, I fear you will shock our guest," said the baron, laughing now, but Claire saw that Mr. Bennett had joined with Lady Sally in the fun. His look of anticipated boredom was gone and he had begun to relax in their company, indeed seemed truly to be enjoying himself.

"Not at all, Lord Oliver," said Mr. Bennett warmly, smiling at Claire in such a way that she knew he was in complete agreement with her. "I perceive that Miss Oliver has some sound views on the subject."

They continued discussing politics happily until the mention of Princess Charlotte's death introduced the topic of succession.

"Such a scramble there has been amongst our aged dukes to marry," Lady Sally said with a laugh. "Lady Sitch—Sitchville—tells me that Kent has been more fortunate than Clarence, who has ended up with a most unpleasant-looking wife. How ill-mannered it was of him to desert his mistress after all these years. It will serve them all right if the Prince outlives them."

"I don't fear that for them," said Mr. Bennett, "since his corpulence is now such that he no longer rides. It must, in the long run, damage his health."

"Well, we shall see who it will be," said Lord Oliver. "There is but a year's difference between Kent and Clarence, and they have both fathered innumerable children. I foresee no difficulty in producing an heir."

"But you know how it is, my dear," Lady Sally reminded him. "Those who produce effortlessly out of wedlock, for some reason do not have the same success when it really matters. I will be content to see one healthy, legitimate child for every ten that Clarence has had with Mrs. Jordan."

Throughout this conversation, Claire had observed Mr. Bennett and noted the amusement on his face. His air of reserve had dropped completely, and it seemed that he had, for the moment at least, forgotten the care that he had appeared to have when he arrived. She was glad to see him blossom in their company. He was immensely enjoying the conversation, the nature of which Mr. Twickenham would not have considered proper to have with ladies present. Right now he was laughing unreservedly at one of Lady Sally's more outrageous remarks.

"I suppose what we really ought to be concerned with," her father was saying, "is what politics each would adopt if made king. For instance, would Kent really remain the radical? We could use a reformer."

"It does not matter much, dear," said Lady Sally with a smile. "He is such a Whig that I'm sure any child he has will become a confirmed Tory. Children always rebel against their parents' wishes. Do they not, Mr. Bennett?"

"Unjust and unfair!" cried Claire, with a laugh. "You can certainly not accuse me of that!"

"Of course not, love," replied her mother. "I was merely testing Mr. Bennett to see which of us he would feel it necessary to support: you because it would be just, or me because of my age."

Claire was doubly pleased to see that their guest knew the only proper response to Lady Sally's teasing—laughter. The lines in Mr. Bennett's face showed that he was accustomed to smiling, perhaps often enjoying the ridiculous that too few people seemed able to recognize. Only rarely had an outsider been able to break into the Olivers' extraordinary intimacy and join in their fun, but this man had penetrated it in a matter of minutes. His broad smile answered Lady Sally's impudence, but as a mark of acknowledgement to Claire, who also displayed a clever tongue, he raised his glass.

"A glass of wine with you, Miss Oliver," he proposed. And as they raised their goblets to their lips, their eyes met and they both smiled. Warmth filled Claire, but whether from the wine or his smile she did not know.

As the evening wore on, the Olivers learned that Mr. Bennett had had a commission in the military.

"You must have been involved in the recent hostilities with Napoleon," remarked Claire who had heard of little else during her season in London.

To her surprise, an air of restraint once more descended upon Mr. Bennett.

"No," he replied, "I was in America."

"Oh," Claire said, her dismay at that reality showing.

Mr. Bennett nodded in her direction. "Very good, Miss Oliver. There are not many young ladies who would even know that we had been there." This was said with a certain sarcasm, barely concealed, for he was referring to the War of 1812, in which the British participated only half-heartedly, greater concerns being elsewhere.

"An unfortunate business," Lord Oliver said uneasily. "You were back too late to join Wellington in Europe, I take it."

Mr. Bennett inclined his head again. "Precisely. My regiment was in the middle of the Atlantic when the duke was at Waterloo." He stopped speaking for a moment, then continued, "After that, there did not seem to be much point in my staying in the military, so I sold out."

"I confess I am curious to see the Americas," said Lady Sally, trying to restore cheer to the conversation, "though of course I never shall."

"It is an interesting place," said Mr. Bennett, and in describing for her some of the things he had seen, he relaxed again. A note of enthusiasm entered his voice when he talked about the democracy there and what effect its success or failure would have on England.

As Claire listened she felt carried away by the emotion she sensed behind Mr. Bennett's words. She felt the challenge he felt, and the eagerness to be part of it.

During the debate that ensued, Claire enjoyed the increasingly friendly conversation that flowed between her parents and their guest. The rector's manner was open and trusting, and the only time that Claire sensed any withdrawal on his part was when reference was made to his cousin or his experience in the military, or to Lord Sitchville and his present position. He seemed to avoid those topics, and when they were mentioned, his countenance became restrained, and she had the impression again of there being some care or disappointment in his past.

When it was time for the ladies to leave the table, her father sent them off with a promise not to be too long in joining them.

Lady Sally could barely wait to enter the parlour before exclaiming, "My love, it is settled! He is simply too good for Lydia. We must find someone else for him. His manner is charming and he is quite handsome; I am surprised that so large a man has such fine features, though certainly his jaw and his brow are quite strong. I declare, I should fall in love with him myself, except that it is not the fashion now. And, after all, he *is* a clergyman. What a pity that such a splendid young man should be without rank or fortune. With a respectable fortune I should consider him worthy of any female of our acquaintance—even you, my darling." Then, turning businesslike, she took up a pen and paper, while Claire sat in a nearby chair, her thoughts, spurred by her mother's light-hearted comments, having taken a turn she had not expected.

Claire shook her head as if to clear it when Lady Sally went on, "We will have to search among our deserving friends for an interesting young lady, for I think our Mr. Bennett is a prize. I hope that Lydia does not fall in love with him or he with her, for I am sure they would not suit, but one never knows. At times even the nicest men have the most peculiar tastes, but I mustn't be so uncharitable. If they are determined on it, we must let it happen."

Claire had to laugh at the speed with which her mother was settling the lives of two people who had not even met. "Remember, Mama, that we know very little of Mr. Bennett as yet, and that Lydia knows even less."

"Right you are, dear. We must get to work before other people in the neighbourhood know him any better. I believe the living at Garby is worth seven hundred pounds a year or thereabouts. That should make a comfortable life for a lady of small fortune." And Lady Sally sat down to make a list of all of her friends' eligible daughters which, due to many discussions of the candidates and many crossings-out, kept her busy until they were joined by the gentlemen.

No card tables were formed since neither Lady Sally nor her husband enjoyed games and their guest expressed no wish to play. Instead, Lord Oliver showed him proudly over his library, which held a great number of books.

"Your collection is an unusually fine one, my lord. Have you found the time to read all of your volumes?" the rector asked.

"Most certainly. My daughter, Claire, has completed them all as well," he added proudly. "It is impossible for me to purchase new ones as fast as she consumes them."

Mr. Bennett looked slightly startled, but he turned and looked at Claire with respect. "If that is the case, I hope you will both feel free to use the library at the rectory as much as you like while I am there. It is a smaller collection than yours, but it has some interesting volumes. By the amount of dust on them, I would say that my predecessor did not devote much time to study."

The baron confirmed this with a bark of a laugh, then thanked his guest kindly. Claire was quick to show her pleasure at the invitation, for she had often wished that Mr. Twickenham had given them leave to explore his library. But when it was plainly evident that he himself did not use it and seemed ignorant of its contents, she and her father had not felt it proper to make the request. Moreover, the man would have been shocked that a young lady should be interested in such a masculine pastime.

"Your predecessor," Lord Oliver explained, "was given to reading *The Gentlemen's Magazine*. His literary enthusiasms led him to learn all about finger rings, genealogies, tombstone inscriptions and antiquities of tavern signs, and his speculations were confined to the existence of swallows in the winter."

Mr. Bennett laughed appreciatively.

The evening was soon over, and their guest having departed, the Olivers retired to bed after congratulating themselves on the acquisition of a new friend.

CHAPTER FOUR

CLAIRE WAS MILDLY SURPRISED that she did not meet
Mr. Bennett at any of the few local social gatherings
she attended over the next many days. He was much
talked about, however, as was the custom whenever
someone new entered the community. It appeared that
not many of the local families had met him yet, although a few gentlemen had paid their respects at the
rectory and some had seen him about town.

Not long after Mr. Bennett came to dinner at the
Olivers', Lord Oliver received an invitation for his
family to dine at Garby House, Lord Sitchville's tem-
porary residence while the manor was being reno-
vated. It was accepted with more alacrity than usual
since the Olivers felt a mild anticipation of pleasure at
the thought of seeing their new friend there.

On the night of the dinner, Claire chose to wear a
white satin evening dress with a bodice snug almost to
the waist and a flowing skirt. Her sleeves, with small
puffs at the shoulders, stretched tightly to her wrists.
A wide white satin sash was pulled round her midriff
and tied just above the waist in back, drawing the skirt
into small pleats. White lace and pearls served as a
flounce, and her slippers were white satin. She paid
extraordinarily careful attention—though she could
not have said why—to the dressing of her hair,

schooling soft curls around her face, while the longer hair at the back was gathered high on her head, except for two ringlets which were allowed to trail on each side. The only touch of colour came from vibrant blue ribbons that were threaded through her black hair to match her cloak. The overall effect was breathtaking, though Claire, with her lack of vanity, did not see it as such.

As the Oliver carriage made its way to Garby House, Claire mused upon the slow pace of life in the country. Extraordinary pleasures came so rarely and life held such a constant sameness that one was forced to simply accept the monotony and wait patiently for expected treats. It also forced one not to build high hopes for pleasure, because disappointment could so easily follow.

Upon their arrival, the Olivers were received graciously as usual by Lord and Lady Sitchville and found a small gathering of their neighbours present. To Claire's immense relief, Lord Babcock was absent, and it was explained that he was not yet up from London; but when dinner was announced, she had to conclude that Mr. Bennett would not be one of the party. This was surprising since Mr. Twickenham had invariably been a guest at all such gatherings.

Claire did not comment on the matter, but during dinner, Lady Sally, who was seated at her host's right, felt it safe to ask, "We do not see your Mr. Bennett here, Lord Sitchville. I hope he is not indisposed."

"No, no fear of that. I invited him, but the fellow said he had business," he replied somewhat touchily.

"Well, I am certain that it must have been extremely important to keep him away from all of us," said Lady Sally, attempting to smooth over his ruffled feelings. But her remarks had the opposite effect.

"The fellow's always busy," he snorted. "Got some damned queer ideas if you ask me." Perceiving the glare on his wife's face at the other end of the table, he remembered himself and hastily excused his bad language.

Too polite to ask what Mr. Bennett's ideas might be and afraid of angering him further, Lady Sally merely said, "I am sure that Mr. Bennett would be more in attendance if he knew that his absence caused you displeasure, since you were so kind as to grant him the living here."

Lord Sitchville looked slightly mollified. "Cousin of my dear friend Avonley. Said I would do him the favour, you know." Frowning once more, he added, "I don't mind telling you, though, that if Avonley weren't such a favourite of mine, I'd try to take it back. The fellow's no better than an Enthusiast!" Lowering his voice to almost a whisper he explained, "A fanatic, y'know. Poor show." He shook his head disapprovingly.

Lady Sally smothered a smile. She had detected nothing of the Evangelical in Mr. Bennett and correctly assumed that Lord Sitchville merely meant that the rector was taking his duties seriously, a circumstance not calculated to please his benefactor.

Lord Sitchville still looked annoyed. "I shouldn't have allowed it in the first place."

At this point in the conversation, Lady Sitchville, somewhat alarmed by the testiness in her husband's voice, addressed the entire company from the other end of the table to ask how they were enjoying their

meal. Lord Sitchville turned to the guest on his left
and no more was said on the subject of Mr. Bennett.

The evening passed slowly as the Olivers had to do
their penance at Lady Sitchville's whist tables. It was
largely uneventful except that Lady Sitchville made a
point of informing Claire that her son would soon be
home, much to Claire's annoyance. The knowing
smiles and significant looks that were exchanged by
many of the guests were exactly the kind of attention
she had trouble bearing.

In an effort to convey her polite indifference she
said in speculative tones, "Lord Babcock must be desirous of returning in time to see the renovations of
your manor." Too late she realized that her statement
could be interpreted as a self-interested request for information. Her discomfort increased as Lord Sitchville gave her an indulgent look.

"That he is, child, as you may imagine. We can
flatter ourselves that Babcock will have more than one
reason to be pleased when he comes home." With the
air of one sparing her blushes, but only too ready to
indulge his own consuming interest, he began talking
about the renovations.

"You will all be invited to a series of parties," he
announced in conclusion, "for which my lady will be
getting the invitations out soon. Hope there'll be
something to entertain you all." With another grin at
Claire he added, "I'm sure a ball will be particularly
pleasing to you young 'uns, eh?"

Claire bore up under this badinage as well as possible, but she was immensely relieved when the time
came to bid their hosts good-night. Perhaps feeling
that he had teased her enough for one night, Lord

Sitchville did nothing more then but compliment her upon the dressing of her hair.

"I can't abide women's bonnets these days. I went to a dinner in London not too long ago, and the women on either side of me had such big hats I couldn't see my food!"

Claire chuckled and parted in a better humour than earlier.

On the way home in their carriage, the Olivers discussed what they had heard that evening.

"It seems our Mr. Bennett does not know how to please his patron," concluded Lord Oliver. "He must be at odds with Sitch over something. I hope it does not cost him much, for Sitch could still make things uncomfortable for him here. He cannot take back the living, I suppose, but it will be a shame for a good man like Bennett to be denied any ambition."

"Perhaps he is not aware of Lord Sitchville's feelings on these matters. About his attendance at these dinners, for instance. Perhaps someone should speak to him about it," suggested Claire.

"That may be the case, but as I said before, my dear, this is Mr. Bennett's affair, and being a reasonable gentleman, he knows what is best for himself," cautioned the baron.

Claire remained silent, not wanting her father to think that she disagreed, but she was unconvinced. It was too rare an occurrence for them to acquire a new friend, and she decided that it was up to her to do something on his behalf. She had no radical plan in mind; she simply felt that a word of caution to Mr. Bennett was called for. It might be a bit presumptuous, but she felt sure that he would take it in the right

light, as timely advice to a newcomer from a person
who was well acquainted with the community. They
were all agreed that Mr. Bennett was the perfect man
for the parish, so why should they not do something
about it?

"It is still astonishing to me," Lady Sally was saying, "that such an attractive man could be related to
Avonley. Why, there could not be two people more
unalike. At one time I could not go to Garby House
without being in fear of meeting Avonley there,
though fortunately, it has been a few years since he has
come. I do not think that Theresa is very fond of him
and I suppose he finds better sport elsewhere. They say
his only passion is shooting. A revolting man!" she
said with a shudder.

"True, my dear," said Lord Oliver. "Who knows
what aberration of nature is responsible for it? We are
very fortunate in the difference, though, for we might
have been saddled with a rector of very mean dispo-
sition."

The Olivers made up their minds to attend the next
Sunday's service to see exactly what it was that was
angering Lord Sitchville, and Claire silently told herself that it would be a good time to speak to the rector.

ON SUNDAY MORNING they made their way to their
seldom-used family pew. It was situated at the front
next to the Sitchvilles' imposing structure, which contained red satin cushions, curtains and even a fireplace inside its high walls. In winter the fires were
allowed to smoke, much to the annoyance of the other
worshippers, but Lord Sitchville, in the rare times that

he appeared, was rendered comfortable enough by them to sleep soundly to the end of service.

The Olivers' pew had enough cushions for comfort and rugs for their laps on cold days, but they had little used it over the past several years, because Mr. Twickenham had driven them away with his inoffensive but pointless sermons.

The church was more crowded than usual, which they attributed to a general curiosity about the new rector. The Willoughbys joined them in their pew, which Sophia and Lydia had been using faithfully, Robert accompanying them when he could be persuaded to do so. Even Lady Sitchville made her appearance, intending, it might have been supposed, to serve as a good example. Lord Sitchville, to no one's surprise, was not present.

Mr. Bennett entered soberly, his visage calm. He read in a deep melodious voice and with a sincerity of tone to which Claire found herself listening with pleasure. The readings over, he returned to the vestry to change his surplice for a black Geneva gown and band before mounting the pulpit, which was on a third tier directly over the clerk's seat and the reading desk. Sconces stuck along the wall provided lighting.

Mr. Twickenham had been careful never to offend with his sermons—and therefore, never to enlighten. Mr. Bennett, ignoring what might be considered bad taste, had the courage to mention Christian teachings about the poor, the justice that was due them, and the consequences of overlooking one's duty towards them. It did not take a thunderous voice or an intimidating manner to make these words offensive to Lord Sitchville, the Olivers well knew. The calm sincerity in Mr.

Bennett's voice was more impressive than any amount of shouting and threats. It was his words, rather than his manner, that had led Lord Sitchville to accuse him of being an Evangelical, for Sitchville would consider them inflammatory.

But Claire was impressed. She left the pew feeling not guilty, only inspired. It was a new experience for her to leave church experiencing any sense of uplift, since Mr. Twickenham had been such an obvious hypocrite. His priestly robes had barely concealed the habit he wore to go fishing, for he spent most of his daylight hours doing just that. The Sunday service was the only duty he performed unless specifically requested and even such requests were not always scrupulously attended to.

As the Olivers were leaving church after service, Claire lagged behind to try to catch a minute with Mr. Bennett, who was standing at the door saying a few words to each person who passed. She happened to reach the door as her uncle Robert was finishing a hurried conversation with the rector. Robert had a somewhat anxious look on his face and Claire was surprised to overhear what she understood to be a request for Mr. Bennett to meet with him on the morrow. It was obvious that the rector had acquiesced, though not without some mild surprise. Uncle Bobby moved on, however, and Claire turned her mind to the task at hand.

"Good morning, Miss Oliver," began Mr. Bennett, greeting her with a smile.

"A very good morning to you, sir," she responded. "And a very pretty sermon that was. I will have you know that we are not used to that sort of talk around here," she added lightly.

"Did you find my sermon offensive?" he asked her, still smiling.

"Of course not," she answered. "It is just that when one is accustomed to Mr. Twickenham, it is quite a surprise to find a sermon which one prefers to a pint of ale."

Mr. Bennett looked amused but puzzled by her statement.

Claire explained herself. "I can see that no one has told you about the occasion your predecessor, already foxed and finding only men in the congregation, offered them a pint in lieu of the sermon." When she saw the dawning comprehension on Mr. Bennett's face, she continued, "And I must say, after suffering through many of his sermons, that I could not blame the men for their choice."

He laughed. "I will engage then, Miss Oliver, to offer you a pint—or a glass of sherry if you prefer—should you find yourself disappointed with mine."

She smiled at him. "Somehow I do not think you will be required to do so. But if the issue comes up with the village men, I should warn you that on the previous occasion, Mr. Squint held out for a quart."

"I appreciate the warning," said Mr. Bennett, clearly quite delighted by the conversation. Then, remembering his manners, he added, "May I thank you again for a most pleasant time at dinner that evening."

"It was very kind of you to join us," replied Claire, perceiving that he had given her the perfect opening.

"We have noticed with regret that you have accepted few other invitations in the neighbourhood."

"Yes, unfortunately. I often have parish business to which I must attend, otherwise I would be quite happy to accept more of the invitations I receive." His tone was one of polite insincerity.

Now that the time had come to make her point, Claire found that it was more difficult than she had anticipated to put her thoughts into words without sounding patronizing, so she fumbled for an angle. "We were most surprised to note your absence at Lord Sitchville's dinner last Tuesday. I imagine that it would be difficult indeed to turn down his invitation."

Something about this speech caused Mr. Bennett to sense that there was some underlying significance to her words. Thinking that it might be enlightening to see what more Miss Oliver had to say, he assumed an air of respectful questioning.

"Do you feel, then, that I was in error in not accepting the invitation?"

Claire, gathering from this naïve question that Mr. Bennett was indeed in need of advice, rushed on, "Not perhaps in error in a social sense so much as in a tactical one. I fully understand your need to attend to the parish, but perhaps you do not fully understand Lord Sitchville's character—what he requires to make him happy." Claire began to falter as she perceived a glint in Mr. Bennett's eye and a stiffening in his manner.

"It...it is presumptuous of me to suggest anything to you on such short acquaintance, I know, but...but..." She'd begun to stutter, but at last blurted out the rest. "I know that he would be greatly pleased if you attended his dinner parties and such."

Claire felt as though she had shrunk in stature. There was no mistaking the coolness in Mr. Bennett's tone when he replied, "Your advice is kindly taken, Miss Oliver. I will certainly take it to heart." And he bowed her out formally.

Relieved to find the conversation at an end and dismayed at its outcome, Claire moved on. There were other people behind her waiting to speak to the rector. She realized that her father had been right when he had cautioned her to stay out of Mr. Bennett's affairs. The rector had certainly not welcomed her advice, and she knew from his response that she had not only presumed, she had offended. She was not at all clear about what she had said to merit just such a reaction from him, but he had made her feel like a foolish little girl.

The worst of it was that she had so enjoyed his sermon, and then talking to him and having him appreciate her humour, that to have caused its reversal was a keen disappointment.

CHAPTER FIVE

THE FOLLOWING MORNING, Lord Oliver suggested that Claire and he ride over to the rectory and take advantage of Mr. Bennett's invitation to use his library. "For it is possible that we may not have the opportunity to do so much longer if the young man persists in offending Lord Sitch," he pointed out. Claire was in no way averse to this scheme since she was ever on the lookout for things to occupy her mind and time, and she doubted that Mr. Bennett would glower at her in her father's company, so they set out in their curricle. The trip was a short one, just over two miles, for the Olivers' estate lay not far from the age and the church was just the other side. Claire ela the reins, as she frequently did when they were together, for her father had taught her to drive with competence.

As they approached the rectory, Lord Oliver, seeing no groom in attendance, instructed Claire to alight and go up to the house while he stabled the horses. He handed her down, climbed back into the curricle and headed for the stables, while she moved towards the house and prepared to wait for her father near the doorway.

The rectory was a Georgian structure which, at this time of year, was beginning to show fresh sprays of ivy

clinging to its stones. It was small compared to the
Oliver mansion, but quite suitable for its purpose.
Claire, who had since her coming-out been there many
times for teas and small dinner parties, noted with
approval the slight changes the new rector had made
in the gardens. Some of the statuary which she had not
particularly liked had been removed, and the gardens
had a softer, more natural look for which she was hard
put to find the reason. As she turned her gaze once
round the entire enclosure, she realized that it was
taking on more the aspect of a park, with the trees and
shrubs being allowed to grow more naturally. This
pleased her, for she had never sincerely admired the
clipping and tailoring of the formal garden.

Claire arrived at the house, approaching as she had
from one side of the circular drive. As she passed what
she knew to be the drawing-room window, she was
startled to recognize Uncle Bobby's voice coming in
excited tones from the inside. Only then did she remember the appointment that she had overheard him
make with Mr. Bennett on the previous day. The
words she was now hearing, which came to her loudly
and distinctly, were uttered with a ring of triumph.

"She says that the sins of the fathers shall be visited upon the sons!"

Mr. Bennett's reply was cautious and questioning,
as though he were as much in the dark as to the direction of the conversation as Claire was herself.

"Yes, Mrs. Willoughby is correct; that is what we
are given to understand. But I am afraid that I do not
fully comprehend what you want me to tell you."

"But that's just it, man!" exclaimed her uncle.
"Don't you see? I haven't got sons! Only a daughter!

The good book doesn't say anything about daughters, does it? So what's the point?''

Claire had to stifle a cry at the stupidity of her uncle's comment, which tickled her enormously, but at the same time dazzled her with its foolishness. She heard Mr. Bennett disguise a similar reaction with a discreet cough before he replied, ''In point of fact, Mr. Willoughby, the Scriptures do not mention daughters specifically there, but it is the general interpretation, I am afraid, that the word 'sons' is used to encompass all offspring, whether male or female. I think you can rest assured that the phrase was not intended to relieve men or indeed women from the consequences of their misdeeds to their children.''

Just then, Lord Oliver caught up with his daughter and they proceeded to the door without a word, although Claire could dimly hear her uncle expostulating in the background. Her father, whose hearing was not as keen, was unaware of his brother-in-law's presence until their paths crossed in the hallway of the rectory. Mr. Willoughby had come out of the parlour with an expression of discouragement but not defeat. When they encountered him, his look became sheepish and he was suddenly in a great hurry to get away. He bade them good-day, thanked Mr. Bennett and took himself off. The baron was a little amused to find him there, obviously thinking that it was the work of Sophia, for how else to explain Bobby's association with the clergy.

From the different looks on the baron's and Claire's faces, Mr. Bennett managed to discern that, of the two, only Claire was aware of what had just transpired, and an amused glance passed between them.

Claire experienced the delicious feeling of sharing a joke, which she had rarely experienced outside her own family, and she was pleased to find that the rector's warmth towards her had apparently been restored. He had either forgotten or forgiven Claire's presumption of the day before.

Mr. Bennett turned to the business of welcoming his new callers and offering them some refreshment, then expressed his delight that they had come to use his library. He offered to show them around and point out works of particular interest, including some of his own books. Lord Oliver seemed reluctant to put their host to so much trouble, but he was quick to put them at ease.

"As a reader, Lord Oliver, surely you will understand the pleasure in sharing a favourite book with a friend," he said.

"I, unfortunately," the baron answered with chagrin, "am more familiar with the displeasure of having my favourite works unread by most of my acquaintance and misunderstood by those who have read them. I hope that you will find my daughter and myself to be more worthy of your attention."

"I have no doubt of that, sir," said Mr. Bennett, smiling at Claire as he did so. "Indeed, I am sure of it." Then he proceeded to give them a tour of his library, encouraging them to browse as long as they liked and to call as often as they could. Lord Oliver was delighted to find some of his old favourites from his Oxford days which were not in his own library, and he settled down to peruse a number of them, preferring his old friends to anything new. Claire was a bit overwhelmed by the selection before her, as most were unknown to her and she scarcely knew where to begin.

Sensing Claire's dilemma, Mr. Bennett smiled at her and asked, "Are you a student of science as well as politics?"

Claire started and then blushed as she recalled her conversation on the night he'd come to dinner. "Not many scientific works come my way," she answered, "since my father is more interested in philosophy than physics and his library reflects his interests."

"Then, perhaps for a change you would like to glance at some of my recent acquisitions about the origin of various life species, one by a Frenchman called Lamarck. I find his theory to be very thought-provoking and I should be interested to see how it strikes you. Of course, if it does not interest you, we will find something else that will."

Claire was completely disarmed by his acceptance of her mental capabilities, and she hastily and eagerly assured him of her interest. She was grateful to him for offering her the chance to learn about something new, something that none other of her acquaintance would consider a fit subject for a woman to read. She took the book he held out and sat down in a comfortable chair to look at it.

"If you and your father will excuse me while I attend to a small matter of business, I will return shortly," the rector said. "I hope that before you leave you will permit me to show you around the garden."

Claire indicated her pleasure at the thought and began reading. The subject was new to her and made difficult reading, but by the time Mr. Bennett returned to the room she was totally enthralled. The rector proceeded to invite Claire and her father to take a turn in the garden. Lord Oliver, however, suggested they go without him, so happy was he with his reading.

"How are you finding the book I suggested?" asked Mr. Bennett as they strolled out a set of double doors that led to the garden.

Unable to keep the enthusiasm out of her voice, Claire replied, "Of course, I have not delved very deeply into it yet, but the little bit I have read is fascinating and entirely new to me. I have always taken the animals and plants around me for granted and have never given any thought as to their origins."

"It is a fascinating subject, one that is being debated hotly these days. You can imagine the opposition coming from the Church. I myself am not at all certain that we won't experience a major upheaval in Anglican theology as a result of these findings."

Claire was impressed. Rarely was she exposed to anyone who was as well educated as she was, but she now had a glimpse of the wealth of subjects to which she had not even been exposed. The thought was exciting, and she began to realize that there was much more to Mr. Bennett than she knew. She regretted her condescension to him on the previous day, although she hoped that he had begun to take it with the proper spirit. Her intentions, after all, had been of the highest.

She was reminded of her uncle's visit to the rectory and she could not refrain from mentioning it. "I could not help but overhear the last part of my uncle's conversation with you as I approached your door today," she said with a twinkle in her eye. "I can see that his understanding of moral matters has not improved in spite of my aunt's attentions.''

Mr. Bennett chuckled and turned to face her. "If you only knew the effort it costs me not to laugh, sometimes quite uncontrollably, when I receive the confidences of some of my parishioners. I should not confess such a thing, but I think you will understand. I must admit that I have never come across just such a one as your uncle, however.'' He became more serious and looked at her quizzically. "Can you think of any trouble that your uncle might be in that would cause some embarrassment to his family?''

Claire looked startled. "Why, no. Have you reason to suspect that such might be the case?''

"Not really,'' he admitted. "It just seemed to me that he was very anxious to find an escape, or justification, or excuse of some sort. There was nothing definite. But I have never been approached on such a matter before, almost as if he were trying to get a clearance or indulgence before the fact. Most peculiar.''

Claire laughed. "Don't worry about Uncle Bobby. He is a law unto himself. He is something of an eccentric, but entirely harmless. He has been irresponsible in the past; I have no wish to be indiscreet about his business, but it is no secret and a number of people around here will tell you if I don't. He loves to muse on the inequities of life, as he perceives them, which is invariably from the point of view of lacking the things he most desires, no matter that he is largely responsible for the present state of his affairs. My guess is that my Aunt Sophia, who is enamoured of the clergy in general, suggested that he call upon you,

and to preserve peace at home, he complied—if you
will forgive my frankness. As to the subject of his
conversation, it is quite likely that he considered it a
topic that you would enjoy, quite the intellectual debate!''

Mr. Bennett laughed again and seemed inclined to
accept her reasoning. Claire was glad that he did not
stand upon his dignity as a clergyman. Having settled
the question about her uncle, she thought to compliment him upon his changes to the rectory gardens.

"I am glad you like them," he replied. "It is never
too early to start making changes if I intend to be
staying here for a time, and as long as I am here, I
want to enjoy the aspect."

His words caused Claire to look at him searchingly,
and as if divining her thoughts, he returned her gaze
and said contritely, "You must forgive my manner to
you yesterday, Miss Oliver. I know that your intentions were generous." He hesitated a moment before
going on, but seemed to respond to her silence with a
sense of trust.

"I'm afraid that I resent the commonly held views
about what is required of a dependent clergyman. You
see, it is with a certain reluctance that I have em-
braced this profession, but having done so, I intend to
handle it in my own way."

Claire looked at him, and the questioning concern
in her expression encouraged him to continue.

"I do not mean to spend my time shooting with
Lord Sitchville and his friends, nor fishing, as I understand Twickenham did. There are things I mean to
accomplish here and they will occupy my time.
Frankly I do not care to sit over a glass of port with

Sitchville and his cronies exchanging ribald stories—I also hear that Twickenham was one to tell his share of stories when in his cups. Nor do I intend to please Lady Sitchville by playing whist at her elbow and complimenting her play. It is not the wealthy here who need my help and I do not intend to waste my time with them. In short, I am starting as I mean to go on."

Claire smiled apologetically at him. "Now I see why my remarks were so offensive to you yesterday, and it is clear that I deserved your reaction." She stopped him before he could protest.

"I have only admiration for your intentions," she went on. "You are quite right, and I was only speaking from the ignorance borne of not having known another clergyman who takes his duties seriously. I must suppose from what you say that you are not ambitious for yourself and that it is of no importance to you to find favour with Lord Sitchville."

Mr. Bennett smiled grimly. "Yes, you've stated it well. And indeed I think that I have quite given over thinking of my own ambitions."

"Well, then, I have only one more suggestion," said Claire gently, "and that is that while Lord and Lady Sitchville, and others of us in fortunate circumstances, may not need your attention so much as the poor, we must all of us benefit by your influence. I hope that you will give us the opportunity to learn from your example."

Mr. Bennett smiled at her, amused yet chagrined as well. "I do not mean to hold myself up as a paragon, Miss Oliver. The occasions I decline invitations are most often ones which I emphatically do not wish to attend. They hold nothing but boredom for me. I accepted your father's invitation with pleasure for the simple reason that I liked him when he called upon me and I knew that I should enjoy talking with him again. I do not mean to be a hermit."

Claire laughed. "I have just been wondering why you decided to dine with us. You must know that it was written all over your face when you arrived that you expected to be bored out of your wits. And if it was not my father you feared, it must have been my mother and me!"

Mr. Bennett looked very surprised to be found out, and he laughed guiltily.

"I will be honest with you. As much as I admired your father from the start, I could not know that my admiration would extend to you and your mother. I have spent many a dull evening in the home of a provincial gentleman and his family due to the constraining influence of a dull wife or daughter. It is only in London that I have come across such intelligent and witty women as yourselves, and those are always many years my senior. Lady Melbourne, Lady Holland— you must know who they are."

Claire blushed at the compliment and then laughed. "I can see you mean to excuse yourself with flattery. We can certainly not boast of being in the same class of hostess as those two ladies."

"No," said Mr. Bennett, smiling comfortingly, "you are not so jaded."

Claire thought it was time to change the subject, and thanking him, remarked that she had better return to her father soon so that they would not overstay their welcome. Denying that this could ever be the case with such charming company as theirs, Mr. Bennett led Claire toward the rose garden where he kindly cut some buds for her to take with his compliments to her mother. They returned to the library, and presently the Olivers set off for home.

What an extraordinary woman, thought Mr. Bennett as he watched them drive away. He could not recall any female of his acquaintance who had her abilities; and on top of that, she was beautiful. He remembered appreciatively the way she had talked about her uncle, with humour but no lack of affection, and with a frankness he had long ago despaired of finding in the gentler sex. There was something else about her, too. He could talk to her on any subject, it seemed, and he was understood. He was very comfortable in her parents' company as well. Lord Oliver was a man he could respect and admire; Lady Sally was an engaging rogue.

He thought about the remarks Claire had made about his influence, not as a compliment to himself, but from another point of view. Surely it was part of his duty to try to get more of the people with income to notice those without, and she was right that he should not neglect that aspect of his work. It was hard to know how best to do it and, up until now, he realized he had been quite tactless. He had simply confronted Lord Sitchville with his omissions and his own strongly worded suggestions for changes. It had not served.

Not very diplomatic, thought Mr. Bennett ruefully. He thought of Claire again. She had begun to restore his faith in the notion that there were other people be-

sides himself who would be willing to take the trouble
to notice the suffering around them.

"Well," he said out loud. "Perhaps I will try it her
way."

CHAPTER SIX

OVER THE SUCCEEDING DAYS Claire thought more than once about her pleasant visit to the rectory. She had found much to regret in the fact that Mr. Bennett had not often permitted himself to be in the company of the local gentry, but she could only respect his reasons. He could certainly make better use of his time if he ignored that set's frivolous and purposeless amusements. She almost envied him the liberty to make such a decision, for as a woman, she did not have licence to ignore society and pursue only her own interests. And even though she enjoyed herself much of the time, she did feel her share of boredom and frequently wished for something more important to do.

Still, Claire knew that her enjoyment of future social occasions would be diminished if the rector were not to take part. She began almost to despair of her situation, for she had never met a *social* equal who had inspired in her so much interest. The gentlemen she knew talked of sheep, horses and bullocks, and conversed about what wind would afford a good scouting day or what course a fox would most likely take upon breaking cover. They inspected the stables and the kennels before dinner, and she rightly supposed that they spent long hours after the meal cracking coarse jokes. And these were her social equals, not the rector of Garby parish.

Claire had to laugh when she thought about her mother's and her own speculations about the new rector—before they had met him. That would teach them to have preconceptions, she thought. No two men could be more unalike than the past and present rectors. She recalled the finely chiselled lines of Mr. Bennett's face, his dark brown eyes rimmed with thick black lashes, the way his smile transformed his whole face and made others want to smile, too. Not at all like Twickenham!

Word reached her over the next few days that perhaps Mr. Bennett had taken her advice to heart. Several neighbours reported that he had called upon them and had accepted invitations to dinner parties and small gatherings of one sort or another. This was confirmed by her Aunt Sophia in one of what were becoming her daily visits to the Olivers.

"Mr. Bennett had the goodness to return Mr. Willoughby's call yesterday," she began. "It so happened that only Lydia and myself were home, Mr. Willoughby being out of the house on some business." Sophia looked round tentatively as though fearing that someone would challenge her on the latter part of her statement, but receiving no challenge, continued, "He is a most pleasing young man, though too tall for my taste. Still, he has a wonderful address. I believe that he was very favourably impressed by Lydia because he expressed his regret that his visit had to be so short due to some duties he was obliged to perform."

Here, at least, thought Claire, Lydia had the grace to blush, though perhaps not for the right reason.

Her aunt went on: "I spoke to Mr. Bennett about the historical merit of our parish church, and I think I have persuaded him to lead a group of ladies on an instructional tour of its older parts. He seemed most willing to do so, and then requested me to be the hostess at a luncheon in the rectory garden. He will provide the refreshments and the servants will be his, but I am to do the planning and see to the guest list. I sincerely hope that you will come."

Lady Sally accepted for both of them and Claire added a remark or two about her interest in the old church, asking when the party was to be.

"Not for a fortnight," Sophia said, "but I assure you that I will need at least that much time to make all of the arrangements. There are so many details to attend to," she added anxiously. Sophia was obviously going to enjoy every minute of every day that she could occupy in playing hostess at the rectory.

Claire, who was anticipating a degree of unnecessary tedium out of this affair, could spare a feeling of pity for her aunt, who seldom had the pleasure of entertaining guests and could not even afford to return the hospitality she received. So she determined to enter into her aunt's plans with as much enthusiasm as possible, and she felt a warm glow of gratitude toward Mr. Bennett for so generously offering her aunt the occasion to give a party. That her aunt thought it was offered because of an attraction he felt for Lydia, Claire was aware. She was not sure if this was the real reason, but if so, it would not be the first time that someone had fallen for Lydia's charms. Unfortunately all her would-be admirers had been frightened off by her lack of fortune, but Claire thought that such a lack would not weigh heavily with a man like Mr. Bennett. Still, she felt that his virtues would be wasted on Lydia and that she would bore him as a wife.

There I go matchmaking, she thought to herself. I am as bad as Mama.

She was abruptly called from her wool-gathering by a comment her aunt addressed to her.

"Claire, you will perhaps be interested to hear, if you have not already, that Lord Babcock is expected back among us at any moment. I dare say that he will be calling upon you himself shortly. Now that is a perfect young man! His address is not to be rivalled, and I have never met a man so mindful of a lady's sensibilities. He will make a wonderful husband; his mama has brought him up so well. I cannot conceive that he would give a moment's worry to anyone." This was followed by a sigh.

Claire knew that her aunt was trying to please her by bringing up Lord Babcock's whereabouts, but she wanted to scream with frustration. She knew that it would be improper for her to tell anyone about her complete lack of interest in the man, though she longed to do so. Besides, her aunt would probably think that she was speaking in a fit of pique, since the whole county thought that Lord Babcock and she should have arrived at some understanding by now. No, best to keep quiet about it and try to turn the conversation.

Claire found it difficult not to grit her teeth as she said, "It will be very kind of Lord Babcock to call on us if he finds the time, but I suppose he will be anxious to go on to the horse races this summer. If you will excuse me, Mama and Aunt, I must see to the arrangement of the flowers for the dinner table." And with that she left the room.

Unfortunately for Claire, her aunt was correct in her unwelcome information, and Lord Babcock presented himself on the front doorstep two days hence. He was announced by the Olivers' longtime butler who could barely hide his disapproval at the proprietary air Lord Babcock assumed upon entering. Indeed, the young viscount looked like the hunter home from the kill, so sure was he of his welcome.

Lord Sitchville's son bore all the appearance of one who had been born to his own title and fortune. He carried himself with a prideful arrogance and vanity, which was revealed by the padding of shoulders and tops of sleeves, and the tails of his frock-coat. Claire suspected immediately from the tight waist of his coat and the stiffness of his walk that he had begun to use stays, for Lord Babcock was naturally stocky and had a distinct paunch. No valet with a conscience could have dressed him, she thought, for jockey boots, though popular, shortened his already short legs, and an overly large stock hid the existence of a neck. His hair was an uninteresting shade of blond and his skin was similarly pale, giving him a bland appearance. Claire, who during his long absences tried to feel more charitable towards him, instantly slipped back into the acute discomfort that he inspired in her.

"Lady Sally—" he bowed over her mother's hand "—and Claire," he said, looking meaningfully at her as he bent over hers. Claire always hated to hear him use her Christian name since it implied a certain intimacy, but she could not deny it to someone she had known all her life. "I cannot tell you how often I have thought of this happy reunion. I am quite anxious that you should forgive what I know must seem a long absence on my part, but I beg that you will understand the demands of a university education, so long and tedious, and of course my parliamentary responsibilities. I can promise you that the educational phase of my life, at least, is now behind me, and I will be much more attentive in the future. You find me humbly in search of your forgiveness."

Claire thought that if anyone looked less humble than Lord Babcock at that moment she would like to see him. How dare he assume that they pined for his return! More than anything he looked to her like the illustrations of Little Jack Horner with his prize plum.

Lady Sally, in trying to hide her amusement at Babcock's pretense of humility, was forced to feign a small cough before she returned his greeting and invited him to be seated. Casting her daughter a conspiratorial glance, she asked Lord Babcock about his trip home. As she and Claire both anticipated, he launched into a lengthy soliloquy about the route he had taken, the condition of the roads, points of interest along the way, the inns he had slept in and the quality of their beds and food, and threaded throughout, his own comfort or discomfort, whichever it happened to be. Claire felt a drowsiness come over her as he droned on and on, and she was reminded of his previous visits, all equally tedious. Finally the story came to an end and he passed on to other matters, asking perfunctorily after Lord Oliver and the Willoughbys, whom he scarcely knew. Just when Claire was fearing that he expected to be asked to stay to dinner, he began to make signs of leaving.

"Oh, we have been chatting so pleasurably that I nearly forgot a commission entrusted to me by my mama," he added as they walked him to the door. "She has particularly charged me to obtain your consent to a dinner party to be given Saturday week in celebration of my homecoming. I must insist that you accept. Your absence would most sadly be felt by all, as I am sure you are aware." Saying which, he gave Claire another meaningful look.

Lady Sally accepted the invitation with as much grace as she could manage, and praying not to detain him any longer, hurried him out of the door.

Claire groaned and fell in a most unladylike manner into the nearest chair. She put two clenched fists over her eyes and then turned her gaze heavenwards in a gesture of mock supplication. "Oh Lord, deliver me of this imbecile!" she shrieked.

Her mother, coming back into the room, laughed, but it was a sound of sympathy. She came and put her arms around Claire and held her head to her bosom.

"Don't despair, love, it will all be over someday. And it may be sooner than you think. Lord Babcock has all the look of a gentleman who is ready to settle down and I think you may receive a proposal sometime this season. You must simply refuse and then finally all this nonsense will be at an end. I know it has been annoying for you, but there has been no way to resolve it so long as he has not spoken. I can promise you that if he should approach your father or me first, we will do all we can to urge him to drop the matter. If he speaks to you first, of course, you will have to handle it yourself, and while it will be most uncomfortable for you, it will be a welcome end."

"I am eager for the chance," exclaimed Claire. "At least there is one thing, Mama. Fortunately, Lord Babcock is a restful suitor. He's the only man I know who would allow me to catch a nap while he is paying court to me. His visits leave me dazed with boredom. Were it not for your subtle Babcock-baiting, there would be no saving humour in them."

"I suppose I should be ashamed of my behaviour," Lady Sally said with a laugh, "but he so enjoys hearing himself talk that I feel I am doing a kindness by giving him an opportunity to do so. After all, when he is a guest in this house it is my duty to see that he has a good time."

"What would I do without you?" Claire returned affectionately. "I can't tell you the number of times that I have given thanks for my two greatest blessings—my loving parents who understand why I am going to refuse Babcock, and my fortune which allows me to do so."

"I am afraid that it is just those two things which are responsible for your having to put up with him. If you were Jane Nobody of no particular fortune you would not be receiving Lord Babcock in your drawing room today," pointed out her mother.

"Well, if I must choose between the lesser of two evils, I had much rather have to put up with Babcock than to lose either you or my fortune," asserted Claire.

"What a pity it is that he is not more like Mr. Bennett and Mr. Bennett like him. That is, it would be so nice if they could just change places. One could very well put up with a Babcock if he were merely the rector of the parish church, but he is quite insufferable as a suitor."

Claire felt a vague unease about such speculations, but without stopping to ask herself why, hastened to change the subject. "I am trusting you, Mama, to see that Babcock and I are never in a room alone together."

"I am afraid that will not stop him if he is determined to make you an offer," Lady Sally replied. "And I am of the impression that he is not the kind of man who takes a hint easily. There will be all too many occasions when he can snatch a few moments of conversation with you privately. But I will certainly protect you as best I can."

"It would probably suit his notions of propriety more if you were never to leave me unchaperoned. I can easily imagine his asking me for my hand while you and Papa were both present."

"And rightly so!" her mother exclaimed, much struck by the idea. "Excellent young man! I should hope that no daughter of mine is suggesting that she would so compromise herself as to receive a proposal of any kind without her parents present. As a matter of fact, perhaps I should speak to Babcock myself. I see no reason at all for you to be present when he proposes."

Claire laughed. "Please don't! He might like the idea! I declare, I have never met a man so unlikely to inspire passion in the female breast."

"Well, my dear," said her mother, becoming instantly more serious and giving her a gentle hug, "when someone does so inspire you—and someone will, of that I am sure—he will be the best of all possible men."

Claire smiled up at her mother, but she released an inward sigh.

CHAPTER SEVEN

ON THE FOLLOWING SATURDAY, as Claire dressed for the evening at Lord Sitchville's, she hesitated for a long while over her choice of gown. Her mother, who had been ready for some time, finally came to her assistance.

"It is not like you, Claire, to keep us waiting," she declared. "Surely you have something suitable for the evening. Why not wear your new yellow gown?"

Claire looked sheepishly at her and confessed, "I know this will sound silly, but I cannot seem to make myself dress for this affair. Undoubtedly, Babcock will take me in to dinner as has been his custom, and I cannot bear the thought that he will think I put on a new gown just to please him." She added somewhat defiantly, "Indeed, I am giving serious thought to wearing something obviously outmoded to put him off."

Her mother gave a sigh as if she were trying to control her exasperation, but looking at Claire's resulting pout she had to laugh. "My dear, you are becoming an absolute ninny over this affair with Babcock. Pray tell me what possible end you could serve by dressing like a dowd for this party."

"Well," Claire began hesitantly, "you know what a stickler Babcock is for fashion. Although I question

his taste, he is well recognized as being knowledgeable about ladies' fashions. I thought that if I could
thoroughly disgust him with my own choice of gown
tonight, embarrassing him in front of his other guests,
he might be so put out that he would drop me alto-
gether.'' Claire made this last pronouncement on a
note of triumph.

Lady Sally was rendered momentarily speechless at
her daughter's outrageous plan; then she was con-
sumed by peels of laughter until she stood in danger of
bursting her stays.

"Why, you little goose," she said, when she at last
got control, "and who else do you think you would
embarrass in the process? What about yourself, your
father, me?''

Claire dimpled, then laughed, too. "I was willing to
sacrifice my own reputation for being in the first stare
of fashion, but I confess I didn't think about you
two.''

"Well, I suggest that you do," admonished her
mother. "Imagine what it would feel like to have every
female eye, and some of the male ones, staring at you
with either anger or amusement. You are not used to
being laughed at, and I suspect that you would not like
it any better than the rest of us.''

"I dare say you are right," admitted Claire with a
sigh. "I suppose I will have to dress according to
fashion to spare the family honour.''

"Yes, darling, you will," said her mother firmly,
"and somehow I don't think you will find that a punishment—'' at this Lady Sally smiled "—so let's not
have any more nonsense, creative though it may be.

Your father and I will be downstairs waiting for you in the library."

Claire could not resist one more joke. "You don't think," she asked hesitantly, "that a train behind my dress, a little damping of the skirt?" Lady Sally fled from the room, laughing. "Clocks on my stockings?" called out Claire. She heard her mother's one word reply, "Dress!" and she desisted.

So Claire dressed reluctantly, but in haste. At least, she thought, yellow was not her favourite nor her most becoming colour. Perhaps Lord Babcock would not be too impressed. Nevertheless she looked very fetching by the time she had completed her toilet. Pale yellow roses descended her white dress in stripes, with a double row of larger flowers round the hem. The sleeves were small puffs, the bodice was fitted almost to the waist, and the neckline cut straight across the breast and vertically to the shoulders. She used combs and yellow flowers to adorn her hair.

As Claire entered the library, her mother looked her over and in a teasing tone of voice said, "It is unfortunate, Claire, that you look quite charming."

Her father, who appeared to be in on the joke, added, "Yes, it is all very sad, for I must tell you that not one male heart will go untouched this evening."

Claire looked at them both sideways from under her lashes. "All right, my revered parents, you have had your fun. It would serve you both right if I did present Babcock to you as your son-in-law!"

Both parents looked momentarily stunned, as if the prospect were more alarming than they could quite joke about.

Then her father said, "Claire, we must be off before I send you back upstairs for that outmoded gown."

At this they all laughed and set off for the party.

Claire was relieved to see, as she entered the room, that the gathering was a fairly large one due to the presence of some house guests as well as the customary neighbours. She hoped that even if she were seated by Lord Babcock during the meal, the presence of so large a company would afford her a little peace afterwards when the gentlemen joined the ladies in the drawing room. She and her parents were pleased to see that, unlike the previous occasion, Mr. Bennett had chosen to come, and he nodded and smiled at them from across the room as they entered. Claire could not help but notice what a fine figure he cut in his pale knee breeches, double-breasted tailcoat, and black and white cravats. His muscular calves showed to advantage in the accompanying stockings, no longer worn as daytime attire but appropriate for evening wear.

Dinner was announced quite soon after their arrival, and Lord Babcock, who had been prevented from greeting the Olivers because of his attendance to another guest, now approached Claire, as she knew he would, to lead her to the table. She thought that she had never seen him look less appealing then this evening, in spite of his fashionable clothing. Strangely, the very artifices he employed to conform his physique to the ideal only accentuated its faults. His waist was tightly bound by stays to counteract an inherent portliness, and the shoulders and chest of his coat were padded, to make him look more powerful. Claire found it particularly irritating that he was affecting a military style of dress when she knew very well that he had never taken part in any campaign.

Having arrived at her side, Babcock made a low bow, offered her his arm and gave her a look as if to say, "You knew you could count on me." As on previous occasions, Claire could only accept the courtesy with good grace, though she wished that he would not make such a ceremony of the gesture. She was aware that in doing so he had drawn many eyes to them, eyes that held knowing looks. She happened to glance over at Mr. Bennett and caught the speculation in his gaze. She looked away abruptly as a flush of annoyance crossed her face.

Much to her surprise, however, Mr. Bennett turned out to have been placed immediately to her right at the table by Lady Sitchville, who was in charge of seating arrangements. Claire had expected him to be placed farther below the salt in such a large gathering, due to his dependent position. The thought crossed her mind that the seating boded well for him, for it indicated that at least Lady Sitchville had a good opinion of the rector. Perhaps, with her influence, Lord Sitchville would feel more kindly disposed towards him. Before she could speak to Mr. Bennett, her attention was claimed by Lord Babcock, who was seated to her left.

"You must know what a pleasure it is for me to see you here this evening," he began in an intimate tone of voice.

Purposely mistaking his meaning, Claire replied, "Oh? Did you think that we would not come? I thought you understood that we had accepted your kind invitation."

The thought that they might possibly have refused it had never occurred to Babcock and he looked taken aback, but he recovered quickly. "You mistake my meaning. But I know how modest you are. That is one of your finest qualities. Do not think I have not remarked it."

"That is very kind of you, my lord, but I fail to see what my modesty, real or imagined, has to do with it. You must know that once we Olivers have accepted an invitation, we always appear, except in the case of illness. Speaking of illness," Claire said, hastening to change the subject, "you appear to be in fine health this evening."

He smiled at her indulgently.

"You and your mother are ever worrying about my health. Indeed, I find it very gratifying to be the subject of so much affectionate concern. Since you mention it, though, I must confess to having had a slight headache before dinner—nothing that you should worry about, but something I feel it necessary to mention, nevertheless. It must have been the excitement attendant upon this evening, tension due to the anticipation of seeing so many dear friends." And with this, he gave her another speaking look.

Trying to ignore it, Claire expressed her devout wish that he was suffering no other discomfort. Lord Babcock hastened to assure her that all was well and that she should have no further worry on his behalf "at present."

Unfortunately for him, Lady Sitchville signalled that it was time to turn the conversation from one dinner partner to the other, and Lord Babcock was obliged to face the older woman on his left. Claire turned to her right, grateful that her first round with Babcock was over. A wave of relief passed over her face, and she abruptly recovered herself upon sight of Mr. Bennett, whose presence she had forgotten during the foregoing ordeal, but not before the rector had caught a hint of the expression on her face. He looked at her a little suspiciously, but as she began to talk, he thought that he must have imagined it.

"My parents and I were pleased to find you here this evening," she began, not thinking of her words of advice to him.

Amused now about that occasion, he replied, "Yes, I have been taking your counsel to heart and have exerted myself more to go out in society, and I must say I have not wanted for opportunities. Everyone has been most hospitable."

Claire blushed as she recalled their words at the church, or rather her words, she told herself dryly. Quite anxious to erase the memory of that occasion, she put his answer aside. "Oh, as to that, I hope you did not tax yourself over what I said. After all, you are quite capable of handling the situation without my interference. Pray, let us say no more on the subject."

Mr. Bennett acquiesced easily because he could see that she was embarrassed. After a short but nervous silence on Claire's part, she asked him about the work he was doing in the area and found him willing to talk about it.

"I have not been here long enough to delve very deeply into the needs of the local poor, as you know, but I have visited all of Lord Sitch...ville's tenants and have a fairly good understanding of their condition." Mr. Bennett did not elaborate on this, and with some

constraint he continued, "I will have a few suggestions to pose to Lord Sitch . . . ville concerning them."

Claire smiled inwardly at his repeated hesitation
over the earl's pretentious new name.

"I would like to establish a school under the Mad-
ras System, if he can be persuaded to set up a fund for
it," Mr. Bennett went on. "Perhaps an impoverished
but reasonably accomplished young woman could be
found to teach in it if she could be provided with a
cottage and a decent income. Thirty pounds a year
would be sufficient. That should not be too much for
Lord Sitchville."

He paused for a moment and looked more closely
at Claire before continuing, "Now that Babcock has
returned I will be interested to see what his opinions
are on the running of the estate."

At the mention of the viscount, Claire felt her customary discomfort, which did not go unnoticed. She
answered dully, "Lord Babcock is quite mindful of his
duty, in estate matters as well as in others."

Finding this statement a bit strange, but not wishing to pry, Mr. Bennett began to talk of other things
just as Lady Sitchville turned to the guest on her left.
Claire smiled at Mr. Bennett and reluctantly turned to
her left once again. And so the evening wore on, back
and forth, while she contrived to keep Lord Babcock
entertained by asking him questions about himself.
This became more difficult as the evening progressed
because she could not ask him about his studies or his
travels, and she ran out of innocuous questions. Babcock did not consider the former to be suitable topics
for a young woman and, to tell the truth, the one or
two times that he had allowed himself to discuss things

with Claire, she had found his understanding to be inferior to her own. She was constantly irritated at the thought of the education that had been lavished upon him and wasted.

Claire was grateful to note that she was so situated at the table that when Lady Sitchville was conversing with the more esteemed of her two guests, Claire was turned toward Mr. Bennett. The circumstance allowed her more lengthy conversations with the rector and longer respites between her bouts with Babcock. During one of her conversations with Mr. Bennett, she thought to ask him something that had puzzled her since the evening of their first meeting.

"If you do not think it impertinent of me to ask, could you tell me what made you go into the Church?"

A look of irritation crossed his face, but glancing at Claire, he relaxed. It was not the first time that someone had been surprised at his choice of profession.

"You stated your question very well, Miss Oliver. I was 'made' to go into the Church," he said dryly. Seeing the question in her eyes he explained further, "As I mentioned to your father, my parents were both dead before I was of an age to begin my studies, and my cousin, who was then the head of our family, wished me to go into the Church. It is quite simple." Mr. Bennett could not keep a certain bitterness from his tone, though someone less perceptive than Claire might not have noticed it.

Although he seemed to have finished his explanation, she hesitated before speaking again, but her curiosity was such that she could not refrain from pressing on. "But there must have been something that *you* wanted to do, wasn't there?"

Mr. Bennett looked down briefly at his hands and gave a gentle snort of laughter, "Oh, of course. There were quite a number of things, and John and I quarrelled about every one of them. Would it not bore you to know what they were?"

Claire smiled and shook her head. "Were they so outrageous that he could not acquiesce to them?" she asked.

"Not at all," replied the rector grimly. "If you knew my cousin, Miss Oliver, you would understand that it was simply because my methods and my wishes were not in accordance with his own. He had early on taken a fancy to see me in the Church. I do not know why. It was certainly not because of any particular reverence for it. I think it was merely that he foresaw my obtaining, with his influence certainly, several good preferments."

Mr. Bennett continued with some sarcasm, "I could always hire vicars or curates to perform the basic duties, you know. I need not have bothered myself with any work. And it is quite possible that I could rise to the position of bishop, always keeping the preferments, of course, to increase my income. It is frequently done."

Claire was beginning to understand his bitterness. It was clear that Mr. Bennett's principles were too high to allow him to enter into the common abuses of Church power. Seeing the concern on her face, the rector resumed a lighter air.

"You must forgive me for harbouring some resentment about my situation, Miss Oliver; it is just not in my nature to live the way John dictates. But to continue, then, if you still wish to hear more, my first desire was to act as my cousin's agent on our family estates. I have a great love for my family seat and could have been happy, I believe, managing it for him. Husbandry is no particular interest of his, so he agreed to allow me a period of trial.

"Unfortunately," he said with a rueful smile, "I grew to be too fond of my cousin's tenants and began demanding they receive better treatment. This incurred my cousin's resentment, for such demands interfered with his amusements. It was not long before he saw that he would have no peace as long as I was around to remind him of his misdeeds, and even though his conscience did not appear to be bothered, his temper was."

Claire could tell, in spite of the rector's attempts to treat it lightly, that the episode had resulted in a bitter disappointment for him.

"My next request," he went on, "and perhaps the most reasonable one, was to be given one of my cousin's seats in Parliament. He has more rotten boroughs than he has snuffboxes and it would not have cost him a penny more than it does to support any other of his members. One of his boroughs has but six voters, and he routinely buys them for twenty shillings a piece. But as you might guess, John had by then realized that I was not likely to vote in a way to please him, so he refused.

"I was down to two choices then, the Church or the military, and considering the events that were taking place at the time, you will not be surprised to know that I chose the latter. I was no less foolish than the rashest hothead and I was anxious to distinguish myself in battle. Again, unfortunately, my cousin had different ideas than I.

"For some reason, John did not want me to take part in the 'unpleasantness' with Napoleon. Perhaps it was closer to home than he wanted me to be. At any rate, he saw to it that the commission he obtained for me was with a regiment that went to the war in America." Claire nodded her understanding, remembering his comments about it on the night of her parents' dinner.

"That was a ridiculous business," said Mr. Bennett with a sad smile. "Fighting a war over an issue that we were ready to back down on, just because they declared war before they got our message. Such idiocy! Still, there is so little love lost in America for our dear George. You do not hear any talk of Old Farmer George over there. They really hate him—perhaps with good reason, though I hope you won't quote me on that. Even so, I got little pleasure out of fighting with men who were but a short time ago Englishmen. Most of our troops felt the same way.

"To tell the truth, I was almost relieved to arrive home too late to participate in the European wars. It would have been much easier to muster some resentment against the French, but I was rather tired of it all by then.

"And that is the end of my story, or at least most of it," said Mr. Bennett, smiling. "It is not particularly brilliant dinner conversation, but you will admit that you asked for it. I hope I did not carry on beyond what your curiosity could tolerate."

Claire opened her mouth to deny any boredom, but her attention was claimed at once by Lord Babcock, who had been chafing under the long conversation with his other neighbour. She could only lift her glass of wine as a gesture to Mr. Bennett before turning, and was obliged to partake of it with Babcock.

Mr. Bennett, too, found it difficult to turn to his other dinner partner, and it was with effort that he appeared to focus on the conversation. He had allowed himself to tell Claire things that he had never discussed with anyone else, and by the look in her eyes, he knew that she had divined the pain behind his recollections, though he had made an effort to hide it. It was remarkable to him the speed with which their friendship was forming, and he cautioned himself that he would need to be on his guard to avoid falling for those understanding blue eyes. He reminded himself of his position, and his expression became so grim as to disconcert the lady on his right.

The dinner was soon over and the ladies rose to move into the drawing room, and leave the gentlemen to their port. For Claire, this part of the evening with Lady Sitchville was the worst, because the assembled women always tried to outdo each other in what Claire thought of as the more negative aspects of their lives. There was a strong competition to see which one had the most illnesses or the weakest constitution, a competition usually won by Lady Sitchville, who as the richest person present was best able to retire for whole days at a time with the vapours, refusing to see all callers. Then those who were parents compared at great length the paleness of their daughters or the fig-

ures of their sons, and the physical weaknesses of both
sexes of offspring.

Lady Sally refused to participate in these contests,
feeling it "ridiculous to be so pleased to have brought
nothing but weaklings into the world!"

Those members who were given to reading at all,
recalled for the benefit of all present the most recent
novel or short story they had read, almost always one
of an improving nature, a tale for the ladies. Everyone discussed the Church, the merits of one set of
sermons over another, the most recent works undertaken—in short, anything of a pious nature that could
contribute to the self-importance of the teller.

Throughout all of this, Claire and her mother usually remained silent, having given up long ago trying
to inject something more meaningful or entertaining
into the discussions. This had earned them the entirely unmerited reputation of being shy or reserved,
which they preferred to being hypocritical.

Sophia Willoughby shone at these soirées, because
when it came to piety, she had no equal. Charitable
works did not require large purses because no one gave
much money to the poor, so there was an equality of
opportunity in this field that allowed her to compete
with the wealthiest. This evening provided many
chances for her to raise the level of attention she com-
manded, already quite high due to the pity she aroused
because of her husband's situation. She used the occasion of having so many ladies of the community assembled to make it generally known that she was to act
as hostess to Mr. Bennett's upcoming picnic and tour
of the church, calling it "a truly sacred trust, I feel, for
it is a great privilege to participate in the religious in-

struction of our young ladies, however humble the contribution." And at this, Sophia cast her eyes downward in proof of her humility.

She received instant affirmation from Lady Sitchville. "It is no wonder that you were asked to assist Mr. Bennett, Mrs. Willoughby, for he must have learned by now of your many services to the poor. Yours and your daughter Lydia's," she added knowingly.

Claire was made more than uncomfortable by the implication of these words, not denied by the pleased flush on Sophia's cheeks. As she reflected, though, she had to concede that it was not an unreasonable assumption on the part of Lady Sitchville, for Lydia had been raised in a manner that made her an obvious choice for the position of clergyman's wife. Who better than a young woman of gentle birth, nonexistent fortune and strict upbringing? At least, with a decent living, Mr. Bennett would be able to support her, and with no fortune of his own he could hardly begrudge her the lack of one. The only thing to say against it all was Claire's conviction that Lydia and Mr. Bennett would not suit, but perhaps that was something unperceived by the two most concerned. Surely it was all too common for one of the partners in a marriage to discover this melancholy fact when it was too late to withdraw. Claire became aware that Sophia was speaking again.

"Without being immodest, I must say that Lydia and I have given a great deal of our time to our worthy poor, and Mr. Bennett has been kind enough to comment on it. Lydia, in particular, goes regularly to the cottages on my dear brother-in-law's estate and reads to the tenants from the Bible. It is so important that these people receive true religious instruction, for we all know what paths they are likely to follow without the proper guidance.'' And with this, all the married ladies gave each other knowing looks over the heads of the spinsters.

Sophia Willoughby was a product of the Society for the Suppression of Vice. Her rather middle-class mother had been quite active in it, and although Sophia herself was not a member, she was a firm believer in its purpose. Its members were dedicated to preventing the free use of leisure time on the Sabbath, the only day that the labouring classes had off. They were pressured to spend this precious time in religious devotion, rather than on amusements. The Good Poor were taught that they would receive blessings as a favour, not as their right. It was a continuing worry to the members just how the poor *were* using their free time, though the same concern did not apply to the Establishment.

Claire stiffened a little in her chair to hear her father's tenants discussed in so condescending a fashion, for they were not so poor as her aunt made out. In fact they were quite well off when compared to others. She also had the feeling, gleaned from her own visits to the tenants, that her aunt's and cousin's visits were not generally appreciated. Though unsophisticated and uneducated, these people seemed to Claire to be perfectly able to choose how to practise their religion—those that desired any—and it was doubtful if being read to inspired them the way it was intended. She was sufficiently riled to break her customary silence, but fortunately, before she could speak, the gentlemen entered the room.

Claire glanced toward the door in time to see her uncle strolling into the room with Mr. Bennett, the sight of which gave evident satisfaction to his wife. As they separated, however, Mr. Bennett glanced at Claire with a look of mixed exasperation and amusement, to which she responded with a smile of complete under-standing. It was difficult not to giggle when one was certain of the type of conversation the two gentlemen had been exchanging; she was sure that it was not what her aunt would have desired.

The smile of pure enjoyment on her face served as an invitation to Mr. Bennett, and he crossed the room to join her just as Lord Babcock, perceiving her, started her way. With a look of mild annoyance at the rector, Lord Babcock turned aside. Claire was sur-prised to note that he did not persevere in his nor-mally possessive and aggressive manner, as she had seen him do so frequently with his social inferiors. She could only suppose that he was deterred in his bad manners by his dislike for the clergy, but she hoped he would not feel offended by Mr. Bennett's natural friendliness to the extent that it would further dam-age the rector's relations with Lord Sitchville.

"Is my uncle desirous of visiting more sins upon his children?" she questioned as she welcomed Mr. Ben-nett to her side.

He replied, with a suitable expression of serious re-flection, "In fact, Mr. Robert Willoughby has been asking me if I could confirm that both Saint Paul and Saint Peter adjured wives to be subject to their hus-bands."

"Oh, dear. I wonder who could have told him that," said Claire anxiously. "Surely my aunt would not have been so foolish."

"No," replied Mr. Bennett, smiling. "I distinctly got the impression that the information was supplied by a member of the servant class, perhaps a groom."

"That must have been Lord Sitchville's new man, Tucker." She frowned. "My uncle seems to have developed a keen respect for him, but I thought it was based on his way with horses, not his knowledge of the Scriptures. It is not an association my aunt would approve of, for obvious reasons."

"If he does no more harm than to quote him Scripture that works selectively to his benefit, the friendship should not be that damaging."

Claire laughed. "I see that he has slipped out of the room, no doubt headed for the stables." She smiled at Mr. Bennett again. "How did you answer him?"

"I had to confirm it, but I pointed out that Saint Peter and Saint Paul also recommended that men be kind and considerate to their wives. The Scriptures are usually quite evenhanded about these things, much more so than most people credit. I find that many like to use the writings for their own purposes, and they can usually find some obscure passage to justify just about any behaviour. Never mind that the passage will be tempered just a few pages further on. The worst is that in focusing where one wishes, one frequently misses the essential message of the whole—love and charity for one's fellow man."

Claire was in such wholehearted sympathy with this sentiment that she wanted to confide in him the ladies' conversation that had preceded his entry into the room, but she decided that it was not her place to expose the others. She began to realize that a similarity of thoughts and opinions was drawing her into a kind of intimacy with Mr. Bennett which made her forget to guard her tongue. Considering his and her relative positions in society, she decided that she must be careful not to be more open with him than would be appropriate. So, beyond signalling her appreciation of what he had said with a demure "I agree completely," she did not allow herself to be drawn into what would have been an enjoyable discussion.

Mr. Bennett moved on with the intention of joining Lord Oliver on the other side of the room, but he halted near the doorway as Robert Willoughby stepped back inside. Mr. Bennett noticed the disappointed look on his face.

"Braving the night air, Mr. Willoughby?" he could not help asking.

Bobby started, "Eh? He wasn't there... I mean, yes. That is, confound it, no!" He became disgruntled. "I don't believe all that nonsense about the night air being unhealthy. Some of my healthiest moments have been outdoors at night." He caught himself and sought to divert the conversation.

Meanwhile, Mr. Bennett had been observing Babcock, who approached Claire as soon as he had taken his leave. There was no mistaking the direction of his attention, so thoroughly did he accentuate each gesture. The rector's expression grew speculative.

Bobby watched him with understanding, and his own recent discomfort led him to an indiscretion.

"I wouldn't get too interested in that direction if I were you," he cautioned. "They have an understanding, if you know what I mean. Since the cradle, they tell me. The way I hear it, she's only waiting for him to pop the question and the knot will be tied. Quite a feather in our caps, I'm sure, to catch a prize like Babcock.''

Mr. Bennett glanced at Robert coldly. He said nothing, but Robert felt the impropriety of his remarks. He rapidly excused himself and joined some of the other gentlemen. The rector glanced back toward Claire and Babcock, then stared vacantly at the room, stroking his chin.

The party, at this point, was being broken up into groups for card tables. Claire was spared a long tête-à-tête with Babcock, which would surely have spoiled the evening, the pleasantness of which had surpassed her greatest expectations.

CHAPTER EIGHT

SINCE THEIR FIRST VISIT to the rectory, Claire and her father had made a practice of calling there twice a week to return their borrowed books and select others. Lord Oliver jokingly referred to the parsonage now as their "subscription library." Christopher Bennett was frequently, but not always, there. The performance of his duties often took him away from home, but on the days on which he was there, he would sit and chat with them both. He seemed to enjoy discussing his books as much as they enjoyed reading them, and they delighted in his company.

For both Claire and her father, the visits to the rectory were a stimulating and welcome change from their relatively uneventful lives. Living year-round in the country as they did, they had little to amuse them beyond visits with neighbours, most of whom Claire had known all her life.

When they saw Mr. Bennett they were always together, and before long the rector came to treat Claire as an equal in their talks as she rapidly proved to be as knowledgeable as her father about the subjects in their library. They quickly became a comfortable threesome, although Claire often sat back and allowed the gentlemen to do most of the talking especially when Lord Oliver's enthusiasm carried him away. She de-

rived a great deal of pleasure just from seeing her father so happy, but she also enjoyed the feeling of
camaraderie. Mr. Bennett treated them both much the
same, except that when he looked at Claire, he always
smiled as if there were something special between
them, something which she had difficulty interpret-
ing.

Neither Claire nor her father learned much about
the rector's personal ambitions during their calls. He
seemed to have thrown himself entirely into the
achievement of his goals in the community, and as the
Olivers learned more about what these were, it became obvious why he had little time to think of his
own life. Having failed to enlist Lord Sitchville's co-
operation in his scheme to begin a school, he persuaded Lord Oliver to provide a schoolroom and a
cottage for the teacher. He undertook himself to pay
the thirty pounds a year for her salary, and Claire
promised to help purchase the materials that would be
needed. The search for a teacher was begun, and Mr.
Bennett was confident of finding one even though the
task of teaching such rustic pupils would be a hard
one.

One of his more ambitious projects was to start a
local newspaper, which the parish sadly lacked. But he
could not find anyone with both the purse and the
courage to begin one. Charges of seditious libel were
common during these years of uneasiness, and the
punishments were stiff. The rector had thoughts of
beginning the newspaper himself, funding it out of his
modest living. But Lord Oliver and Claire strongly
urged him to abandon the idea, for they knew that
Lord Sitchville would take grave offence and would

not hesitate to report him to the authorities if there were anything published slightly uncomplimentary to the present government. And they both knew that there would be!

Mr. Bennett agreed to drop the idea for the time being, because he had many other things to occupy him, but they knew that he would resurrect it if he became frustrated in his other endeavours.

During the week following the dinner at Garby Hall, the Olivers were spared the daily visits by the Willoughby ladies because Sophia was busily preparing for the tour of Garby church and the picnic at the rectory. The invitation list had been expanded to include the gentlemen, in response to Lord Babcock's return and his expressed interest in the affair. As the end of May approached, the allure of an outdoor entertainment increased and there were many more who looked forward to the event.

Babcock had offered to escort Claire and her mother, but Lord Oliver's inclusion in the outing allowed them to refuse gracefully, and he proposed accompanying his mother instead. Consequently, it was with Lady Sitchville in tow that Babcock arrived at the old church door some minutes ahead of the Oliver party.

Sophia Willoughby was standing outside the low stone wall of the churchyard, greeting guests with a proprietary air. She beamed with pride upon spying the new arrivals.

"Lady Sitchville, Lord Babcock, how kind of you to join our little gathering today. You honour us," she began obsequiously.

This speech could not have been better composed to delight Babcock, who had such a high opinion of himself that flattery to him always had the ring of truth. Deciding immediately that Mrs. Willoughby was a kindred spirit, he bowed and proceeded to deliver a flowery speech about the occasion, which he was sure would be properly appreciated. Before he had come to the end, however, Lydia, who had been taking a leisurely turn around the building on the arm of a friend, came into view.

Lord Babcock saw her and stopped in midsentence.

She had put on her finest day dress for the occasion, a pale blue muslin sprinkled with pink roses, with a tight, high waist. White ruching, starting on each shoulder, descended low across the bosom and circled high round the neck, then again at the cuffs and in seven rows round the hem of the skirt. The tight lacing of her youthfully plump figure gave her the appearance of voluptuousness above and below the waist. On her head was a pink straw bonnet with pale blue, silk-edged flowers and ribbons. The blue was as pale as the blue of Lydia's eyes and the pink was as pale as the colour in her fair cheeks. To Babcock, she was the picture of perfection.

For a moment, Lady Sitchville and Mrs. Willoughby waited patiently for him to resume, supposing him to have lost his way through a speech that was becoming more intricate with every phrase. But when he did not recover, the silence among them became embarrassing. Sophia smiled nervously, not wishing to put herself forward, but Lady Sitchville uttered a sharp, "Babcock!"

He started as though unaware of where he had been, then stammered an apology and tried to take up where he had left off, but he was unable to keep his eyes from straying towards Lydia, who had reached the doorway. By this time, both Sophia and Lady Sitchville had discovered the cause of his peculiar behaviour. Sophia was astonished, but gratified; Lady Sitchville's reaction was less clear. She was stunned to see her beloved son behave in such a manner; she had not believed him capable of such strong emotion and was not sure that she approved of it. At the same time, she acknowledged Lydia's attractiveness and approved of her ladylike manner. Unsure of her own feelings, she was unable to react quickly enough to prevent an introduction on the spot. As a group, she, Sophia and Babcock had begun to approach the door to the church and, as they reached Lydia and her friend, an introduction was inevitable.

Mrs. Willoughby proudly presented her daughter, not forgetting to include her friend. Babcock bowed properly to them both, but his all-too-evident attention to Lydia was enough to cause that young lady to blush becomingly. Lady Sitchville, remembering Babcock's impending engagement to Claire, gave Lydia a distant smile, and with the help of Sophia, managed to sweep the young people apart.

Lady Sitchville and Lord Babcock moved on to accept the rector's greetings as he detached himself from another group of guests. At about the same time, the Olivers arrived. The Willoughby ladies met them at the church wall again, but it was evident to the new arrivals that Lydia was overcome by some emotion which her mother was endeavouring to ignore. This was so contrary to Sophia's usual attention to her daughter that they could not help but remark upon it, but both ladies assured them that all was well.

Claire observed upon entering the nave that Babcock had already arrived with his mother, and she inwardly cringed in expectation of his normal attentions to herself in front of so intimate a gathering. Surprisingly, however, he seemed not to notice her arrival until his mother pointedly indicated Claire's presence to him. He started visibly and then advanced dutifully upon her with a fixed and pensive smile on his face. Mrs. Willoughby had conscientiously kept Lydia out front with her to greet other guests.

Soon everyone was present and the tour began, with Lady Sitchville on Mr. Bennett's arm and Claire on Babcock's. In spite of her uncomfortable situation, Claire found herself enjoying the tour, for Mr. Bennett proved to know a good deal about the building, given his short term in the parish thus far. Some of the information she knew already, having taken the trouble to learn something about her parish's history, but she enjoyed hearing him tell it. He had a low melodious voice that was pleasant to the ear and, in spite of its subdued nature, his enthusiasm carried through. He did not seem to be unduly proud of his own connection with the place, but he had a strong appreciation for its history. His lecture was informative without being pedantic, and consequently, even those who had attended in order to be seen rather than to learn became interested. Claire was pleased to see that Mr. Bennett's attitude toward Lady Sitchville and Lord Babcock was polite and patient, though constrained. It was impossible not to be impressed by the confidence he had in himself, which could allow him to treat his patrons with no more than the natural courtesy he would have shown to anyone else.

The tour went on for about twenty minutes with anecdotes thrown in about its establishment in the twelfth century, confiscation of Church property under Henry VIII, and the Reformation. Mr. Bennett timed his lecture so as not to stretch the listening tolerance of his audience, knowing that a good number of them had little interest in the subject. Most of the ladies by this time were ready to sit down and partake of some refreshment, so Mr. Bennett and Sophia Willoughby led the party back to the rectory lawn where the servants had set out trays with food and drink.

During the tour of the church, Lord Babcock had regained some of his sang-froid, but Claire could not help noticing that he was mildly distracted, not at all his usual attentive self. Her own interest in the rector's talk kept her from seeing the surreptitious glances Babcock was throwing in Lydia's direction, and he conducted himself perfectly on the way to the rectory, so there was nothing specific to which she could tie his behaviour. They were joined by Claire's parents on the lawn where they had seated themselves, and the gentlemen left to obtain refreshments for the ladies.

"I declare," said Lady Sally when the gentlemen were no longer within earshot, "I have had enough of my dear brother's wife for one day. She is so overjoyed at the success of her little party that it has gone to her head. She is handing down precepts left and right to anyone who will listen. She would have made a fine rector's wife, but thank heaven she is not this one's or we should be obliged to put up with this more often. Do you suppose she is preparing herself for the role of mama-in-law instead?" She laughed conspiratorially.

Claire smiled, but found it impossible to be as amused as her mother was by such a picture. "I suppose it is possible," she allowed, "but somehow I cannot see Mr. Bennett and Lydia as husband and wife. They do not seem as though they would suit."

"I understand your point, my love," said her mother with a sigh, "but after all, they are each of them destined for such a marriage, if not with each other, then with someone similar. This might be the best opportunity Lydia has for making a good match. She certainly could not do better for a husband, for a more attractive and likeable man does not exist. And Mr. Bennett is of an age to be looking for a wife to help him with his duties. It would certainly please Lord and Lady Sitchville for him to marry, and it would not be charitable of us to seem to oppose the match, just because we consider Lydia's mind to be inferior to what our friend deserves. Men's tastes are not always so easy to understand in this respect, and Lydia is, after all, a very attractive girl. Now, here comes your father. I wonder what can have put such an expression of disgust on his face."

Claire saw that indeed her father did look remarkably annoyed for one who was usually in such gentle good humour.

"What can that woman be going on about?" he demanded as he joined them. "'A lady would not wish' to do this, and 'Of course, ladies do not' do that. As if a lady might not do exactly as she pleases! What on earth does she mean?"

Claire and her mother laughed. "I suppose you must be speaking of dear Sophia," said Lady Sally. "She is insufferable today, isn't she? It serves you right to be suffering her now, though, because you are so quick to hide in your library when she makes her usual visits to us. Claire and I are more used to this kind of talk, not that we like it any the better."

Claire explained, "I think, Papa, that when Aunt Sophia refers to a 'lady,' she means a woman who comports herself in a certain delicate or ladylike fashion, rather than someone born to the position. It seems to be the prevailing definition these days."

"I suppose there are some for whom such a definition provides the only entrée," said her father uncharitably, "but if it means that my daughter may not read a book, they will never get me to accept it."

Both mother and daughter laughed again, but they were soon joined by Babcock, who put an end to their shared amusement.

Babcock had been exceptionally long in returning with Claire's luncheon, a circumstance owing to Lydia's being stationed not far from the serving tables. He had managed quite skilfully to fall into conversation with her, though her downcast eyes and whispered responses had made it more or less one-sided. This did not dismay Babcock, however, who saw her modesty and restraint as congenial qualities approaching his ideal of womanhood. But he abruptly remembered his social duties and returned to Miss Oliver's side with flushed cheeks, a feverish eye and an excited manner. Lady Sally was commenting on his feverish appearance when Mr. Bennett strolled over to their party.

"I quite agree, Lord Babcock," he added with an exaggeratedly concerned air. "I hope today's heat has not spoiled the entertainment for you. Perhaps you would care to rest inside while I conduct Miss Oliver on a tour of the garden." And he casually bowed in Claire's direction.

Babcock was on the point of refusing when he glanced at Claire. For the first time in his life, he really looked at her. She was pretty, yes, and graceful. And she carried herself with the assurance of a lady. But there were times when she made him feel foolish, and she never looked at him with the respect he had seen in the eyes of the gorgeous creature he had met today—the beautiful girl in pink and blue who was now up near the house.

An unmistakable light glinted in Babcock's eyes. "Ye-e-es," he stammered, eagerly magnanimous, "that might be a good idea. I cannot think what has come over me, but perhaps it is the heat. I am reluctant to give up the pleasure of Miss Oliver's company, but I think today she must find me a poor companion. I would be grateful to you for sitting in my stead until I can prove more worthy of her attention."

Babcock's words drew a variety of reactions. Mr. Bennett, both surprised and grateful for his easy victory, smiled and offered Claire his arm. Claire's parents looked shocked at Babcock's eager relinquishing of their daughter, finding it so unlike his normal behaviour that they began to suspect that he really was ill. Claire felt a faint twinge of annoyance at the manner in which he had expressed himself, but she was so happy to be released from an anticipated period of boredom that, after a moment's hesitation to fully understand her good fortune, she sprang lightly to her feet and accepted Mr. Bennett's arm. They strolled away as Babcock excused himself and headed back in the direction of the house.

"I hope you do not mind my interference," began the rector, with a studied air of disinterest, "but Lord Babcock looked decidedly unwell. I thought I might be of some service."

Claire was so happy to be free of Babcock's company that she could not keep a properly serious expression. "On the contrary, we are all grateful. Babcock frets constantly about his health. I dare say the heat was bothering him, but he was too polite to give in to it if it meant leaving someone unescorted and neglecting what he considers the proper thing to do. He was obviously happy to be released from his obligation," she said gaily.

A smile lurked around the corners of Mr. Bennett's mouth. Certainly, he thought, no one could look less like an abandoned female than Miss Oliver. With her beaming face and lilting walk, she put him in mind of a freed bird. He began to wonder if there was something less than what was whispered about Lord Babcock and Claire Oliver.

As they strolled, they chatted pleasantly. Claire took the opportunity to compliment him on his lecture in the church, and he had a willing listener for the facts that he had uncovered but omitted from his tour.

"You seem to know a great deal about architecture, Mr. Bennett. When have you had time to study it amongst your other subjects?" she asked.

The rector smiled sheepishly. "I am afraid that I cannot take much credit for that, Miss Oliver. Perhaps I have not informed you fully about my background. Suffice it to say that my name, my entire name, is Christopher Wren Bennett."

Claire was startled, "You mean that the great architect was one of your...?"

He gave an amused shake of his head and corrected her before she could finish. "No, no relation. It is simply that my mother came from a Wiltshire family which had long appreciated the work of Christopher Wren, and my father was something of an admirer, too—he must have been because he allowed her to name me after him. I was encouraged to learn about architecture as well, but I showed no talent for it. I cannot draw a straight line even with a rule. However, I don't think I disappointed my mother too severely; she always gave the impression of being satisfied with me."

Claire had to laugh at his tale, and she privately told herself how rare it was to find a man who could admit cheerfully to his own shortcomings.

As they rounded the corner of the house, still conversing happily, they came in view of Sophia who spied them and immediately set upon them.

"Oh, there you are, Mr. Bennett!" she exclaimed. "I was just talking about you, wondering what your opinion would be of a little prayer I would like Lydia to say each night at bedtime. It goes like this..." And, before Mr. Bennett could avoid such an inappropriately timed revelation, she took an elocutionary stance, bowed her head reverently and began, "Oh,

Lord, in *sin* was I conceived, please make me free from sin.''

Claire, who had been watching Mr. Bennett's face, saw his expression change from mild annoyance to real anger. Then, as her aunt raised her eyes, he rapidly feigned surprise and shock. Before his attitude had time to register with her aunt, he seized the woman's hand and bent to kiss it.

''Dear lady,'' he whispered in hushed astonishment, ''I had no idea! This comes as the gravest shock to me. But have no fear. God is merciful in his forgiveness. And of course, you may rely completely upon my discretion.''

Claire gasped as the meaning of his action and words sank in. Mr. Bennett looked at her swiftly, then wasted no time in whisking himself and Claire away around the corner of the building again, still managing to take leave of her aunt with a suitably sympathetic gesture, before the full import of what he had said occurred to Sophia. Claire's last image of her aunt was one of someone stunned, confusion and dawning horror vying for supremacy.

As soon as the rector had got Claire sufficiently far enough from the house to be neither seen nor heard, he let go of her arm and turned to look at her. From the expression on his face she could tell that he was already chastising himself for what he had done and was waiting for her reaction. Claire, who had nearly burst with embarrassment and mirth, broke down and laughed as quietly as possible until the sides of her head ached. In view of this, Mr. Bennett had to laugh, too, but it was clear that he was ashamed of himself.

"Please forgive me, Miss Oliver," he said, putting a halt to their laughter. "That was cruel of me. I ought to maintain better control of myself. The truth is that I have been finding it increasingly hard to deal with your aunt's piousness. I am always angered when someone labels as sin the perfectly natural expression of love between husband and—" Abruptly, Mr. Bennett seemed to realize the impropriety of his words and recall to whom he was speaking.

Claire felt the hot flush of embarrassment stealing over her face. She was annoyed with herself for being so missish, but the truth was that she could not discuss the marital bed objectively with this particular friend, with whom she had discussed so much. For the first time, she really noticed the strength in the line of his jaw, the musculature of his neck almost hidden by his neckcloth, and the broad expanse of his chest. The warmth of her blush seemed to spread through her body, causing her hands to tremble slightly. When she spoke next, her voice was husky.

"Of course, it was a positively shocking thing to do, but I am sure she deserved it. We all of us have found Aunt Sophia difficult to support today. She has been inordinately pleased with herself, and her resulting officiousness is too much to bear. You, who have had to put up with her all week, must have had your patience tried beyond endurance."

"It is kind of you to defend me, but it is doubly worse that I should have played such a cruel trick when she has been so happy. She did all the work for today's gathering, you know. She really has been most helpful and kind."

"And it was you who gave her that pleasure," declared Claire stoutly. "You must know that she has done no entertaining since she arrived here, given the size of their cottage and their serving staff. You have done her a great kindness by giving her the opportunity."

This only served to make the rector look more chagrined, but he smiled. "It won't do, I'm afraid, Miss Oliver. You see, I had not the good motives you would attribute to me. The tour and the party were her suggestions and I could easily see that she would be willing to play hostess. I fell in with the plan merely because it would allow me to pay back the invitations I have received with the least inconvenience to myself."

"Well," Claire began, but she could think of nothing else to say in his defence. Perceiving that he was at least amused by her attempts to excuse him, she said, "I can see that you deserve all the censure you are asking for, then, but I suppose you will be punished sufficiently by the dread of your next meeting with my aunt."

He winced. "Yes, I had forgotten about that. But it won't be the first time I have brought this on myself. I have something of a hasty temper, and my tongue has been let loose more than once. I really have no business being in the ministry." Something of his earlier anger reappeared. "It is just that people waste so much valuable time on such unimportant matters. If they were just aware of how much true wrong there is... But I guess they are *not* aware of it and that is exactly the problem. Of course, most people do not want to know about anything unpleasant, and those who do, do not care."

Claire found his words a bit confusing, but she could see that he was preoccupied with some thought, and so said nothing. For a moment he seemed to forget that she was there, for his eyes had a faraway look and his brow was furrowed as though he had some particular problem to solve. As she waited, he remembered her presence with a start and apologized for his silence.

"It is quite all right," responded Claire. "But I wish you would tell me if there is anything particularly troubling you—that is, if I can be of assistance."

He began to say no, but rethinking, he looked at her speculatively. "Perhaps this is something you could help me with," he answered. "I wonder if you know anyone, among your servants, for example, who might understand enough Anglo-Saxon dialect to help me to understand what someone is saying, and to explain my words in the same dialect."

"I think that I can help you with that," said Claire, a perplexed look on her face, "but it might be best if you could explain to me what this is about."

"Yes, of course," he replied. "It is no secret. Just two days ago, I was walking in town when I happened to find a small boy trapped in a mound of dust. It was actually filth which must have been raked there over several weeks, and I do believe the child would have suffocated if I had not seen him. As it was, he was barely distinguishable from the pigs which were scavenging at the bottom."

The rector cleared his throat and frowned. "I pulled him out by the heels and found him to be a small, grossly undernourished boy. Impossible to tell his age, but I suspect from the scarring on his knees and his elbows that he was employed for some time as a climbing boy. He was too weak to protest my carrying him, but it was easy to see that he was terribly frightened.

"I inquired of passersby until I found someone who knew him and could tell me where his home was. There was no trouble to find it, but as his mother was obviously as frightened as the boy by my being there, I did not stay.

"Yesterday, I thought it best just to stop by to see how he was doing, but when I got there I found him on a rough sort of bed in the corner looking very ill. The problem is that his mother speaks and understands only this local dialect, and as a result I cannot make her understand that I do not mean to hurt the boy—and certainly I do not understand anything she says."

Claire looked at him curiously. "What do you mean to do?" she asked.

"I don't know," the rector replied. "But there must be something that can be done for the boy. He cannot just be left the way he is. It looks as though his mother has not been near him, almost as though she expects him to die and has resigned herself to it." Mr. Bennett became aware that Claire was regarding him fixedly. "Why are you looking at me like that?"

She responded, "It is just that you never cease to amaze me. She probably does expect him to die. You must know that most people are afraid of coming near any sick person, even their own children. He will be left to himself and allowed to die if you do not do anything." Then she added, "Mr. Twickenham boasted frequently that he had never entered a sick person's cottage. He seemed to think it a virtue."

"I will be very grateful to you, Miss Oliver," said Mr. Bennett warningly, yet with a smile playing about his mouth, "if you cease comparing me to Twickenham. It is a very lowering thought that I am occupying the position once held by him. I had rather not be reminded that we are supposed to be of a kind."

Claire laughed. "I do not think you need regard it too closely. No one is likely to confuse the two of you."

"Well," said Mr. Bennett, "getting back to the business at hand, can you think of anyone who would be likely to help me?"

"Indeed I can," said Claire cheerfully. "I know just the person. My own nurse used just such an old dialect as a child and I am sure she would be happy to help you. She will be the best person to send, too, for she will be able to tell how sick the child is."

He looked at her doubtfully. "Don't you think she might be offended if you ask her to do this? When I said that this child was hard to distinguish from a pig, I was only partly joking."

"I would be very much surprised if he had seen water and soap in months," agreed Claire. "But do not be concerned about Nurse. To her, a child is a child, and if he requires a good bit of scrubbing she will be all the more pleased. Many a time have I heard her express a wish to get her hands on some of these urchins."

Mr. Bennett laughed. "She sounds just the woman for the job, then. Tell me where I might find her and I will take her there tomorrow."

Claire did not answer him at first. An idea had just sprung to mind, but she kept it to herself and instead merely said, "No, I think you had best let me tell her about it. Then I can send my groom to fetch her and come to you with the carriage. If she cannot come for any reason, I will send you word this evening."

"A very handsome offer. Thank you," replied the rector. Then they both decided that it was time for them to return to Mr. Bennett's guests and for Claire to be off with her parents.

As they approached the others, Claire suddenly remembered Mr. Bennett's last words to her aunt Sophia.

"I do not think that we should appear to have enjoyed ourselves too much," she said in a low voice, "or my aunt might think that it was at her expense."

"No, confound it! You are right," Mr. Bennett said, and they schooled their features. He did his best to look abashed and concerned, and Claire looked agitated, as though her maidenly modesty had been offended.

Aunt Sophia, for her part, had been wondering how on earth she could face Mr. Bennett again. How could he have mistaken her meaning in such a way? Underneath her shock and humiliation was a tiny, lurking suspicion that perhaps he had understood her, after all; but reason told her that it could not be so. It was of the utmost urgency that she correct his mistake, although she could not bear the thought of approaching a subject of such delicacy. Consequently, when she saw Mr. Bennett and Claire return to the house, she looked at them with trepidation, but their facial expressions put her mind at rest.

Both of them looked ill at ease. There was not the slightest possibility that two people with that degree of tension visible between them could have been sharing a joke at her expense. Claire must have taken on the onerous task, for one of her tender years, of setting the rector right. When Mr. Bennett glanced up and saw Sophia, he looked embarrassed and ashamed. Sophia blushed slightly at the recognition, but felt not the excruciating embarrassment that she had expected.

Claire looked quite upset. Poor child, thought Sophia. It must have cost her niece much discomfort to explain her aunt's meaning to him. The whole episode was most distressing! Perhaps, Sophia thought, she should alter the words of that prayer if they could be so grossly misconstrued!

CHAPTER NINE

THE NEXT DAY, not having received word to the contrary the night before, Mr. Bennett was ready to receive Claire's old nurse, when he heard the sound of coach wheels in front of his house at eleven o'clock. He strolled out to the front prepared to join the woman and her attendant in the carriage, but upon reaching the drive he saw to his astonishment that it was Claire and not a groom who was driving.

After a moment's hesitation, he greeted her, smiling grimly. A small, upright woman was seated in the back, her disapproval showing in the rigidity of her posture. Claire presented her to him as Nurse Sutton, and he smiled graciously for her benefit. Then, turning back to Claire, he spoke kindly, but authoritatively.

"You need not have troubled yourself to bring Nurse Sutton to me, Miss Oliver, but I assume that your groom was otherwise employed. I will be happy to drive you to your house if you will give me the reins."

Claire could not suppress a smile.

"I will be happy to let you drive if you prefer, Mr. Bennett, though I must tell you that I am quite capable at handling the reins." She paused momentarily, then stated firmly, "And I have every intention of accompanying you on your mission."

"I do not doubt your capabilities with the reins for a minute," replied Mr. Bennett, trying to preserve his air of sternness, but finding it very hard not to respond to those engaging blue eyes. "But I cannot let you accompany us. It would not be appropriate."

"When I have Nurse with me?" questioned Claire, in a tone of disbelief. "I can't believe that even the strictest critic would say so."

The rector cleared his throat and looked at her ominously. "I was not referring to the propriety of our being together, madam, as you well know. It would not be proper at all for me to take you on a call to the hovel in question."

"I have the permission of my mama, sir, so you cannot possibly object," said Claire primly.

Mr. Bennett looked at Nurse for confirmation of this.

"It won't be no use, sir, tryin' to talk any sense to 'er," this lady replied with glaring looks at Claire's back. "She's that headstrong, she is. And her ladyship ain't no better. A pair of 'em, as what ain't got no sense to be doin' the business they do. But it won't be the first time what she's put herself in where she's not needed and where she's like to catch her death, so don't go blamin' yourself."

Claire laughed warmly at this speech, but then voiced her objections. "You really should not speak of me so to Mr. Bennett, Nurse, or you will have him thinking that I will be terribly in the way. And you know very well that I can be useful."

The old nurse agreed reluctantly, but there was pride in her eyes. "I will give her this, sir, she's mighty good in a sick-room. She was right helpful when them Cratchet twins had the fever, but she had to go and get it herself, then—a light case it were, thank the good Lord—but it wasn't enough just to help out a little, and you should've seen her with—"

"That will be enough, Nurse," Claire interrupted, her face turning pink with embarrassment. "You must not bore the rector with descriptions of my spots. He will have quite a pretty picture of me," she said, laughing.

By this time, Mr. Bennett had realized that he must give in. He climbed up beside Claire in the carriage and gently took the reins from her.

"No, please, Nurse. I would love to have a description of her spots," he said teasingly. "I am sure they must have been charming."

Claire protested loudly, "You are not to do anything of the kind, Becky," she said, reverting to the use of her nurse's name. "You are to remember your loyalties and your affection for me, and not to respond to any of this gentleman's questions without my permission."

The nurse did not respond to this interchange, perhaps disapproving of the tone, but Mr. Bennett laughed with enjoyment and flicked the reins for the horses to start.

They drove on for a while, chatting harmoniously. From the direction they were taking, Claire guessed that the boy's cottage must be somewhere on Lord Sitchville's estate, but she refrained from comment as Mr. Bennett drove confidently, obviously knowing the way. He was good with the reins and complimented her on her horses, which she knew to be a fine pair.

Before she could respond, though, he brought the horses up short at the sound of a distant gunshot.

"That sounded as if it came from the village," he remarked with some alarm. Then, seeing Claire's demure posture and amused expression he relaxed and drove on.

"I can see that you are about to explain it all to me, Miss Oliver. Don't tell me that I have a deranged parishioner who fires shots from a shop window."

"Of course not." She giggled. "It was just Lady Sitchville."

"Oh, better yet!" he exclaimed. "A deranged patroness!"

"Now don't be foolish!" Claire laughed and then made an effort at primness. "I did not mean that Lady Sitchville fired that shot. You know that I did not," she protested as he began to correct her.

"It is simply that she has bribed the coachman on the mail to fire a shot if there is any news of worth from London. You must know that she prides herself on always being the first to have any news that could possibly be of interest. When the shot is heard up at their house, someone will be sent quickly to the inn to find out what it was for. It will most likely be about the Duchess of Kent's confinement. I believe that she was due about this time, and Lady Sitchville is particularly interested in royal births. We will be given the news at the soonest possible moment and I will be happy to pass it on to you."

Mr. Bennett thanked her profoundly and they continued onward, both well content in each other's company.

The hovel in question was soon reached, and Claire saw immediately that Mr. Bennett's concern for her had not been unjustified. As she descended from the carriage with the help of his hand, she could not help letting her eyes show some alarm. Mr. Bennett merely gave her a look as if to say, "I told you so," and led her to the door.

The structure was the meanest of cottages. It was made of nothing but mud and straw, with bits of glass or old, cast-off windows stuck in the mud walls to admit light. The entrance was a small opening formed by odd pieces of wood, barely held together.

The three grim-faced visitors presented themselves at the door and found the mother of the boy within. She was dressed in a threadbare linen skirt and large checked apron that were now little more than rags. There was fear in her face as she retreated into the hovel, and she seemed to be pleading with them to leave, but to Mr. Bennett and Claire her words were almost incomprehensible.

"Becky," Claire said urgently, "you must make her understand that we are not come to hurt her and that we would only like to help." The nurse then spoke to the poor woman in a way that was obviously understood, for the woman stopped pleading and listened with less fear in her eyes.

Claire looked around the room and took note of the poverty. The only furnishings were some boards nailed together to make rough tables and chairs. In a remote corner of this small space was a bed of straw on which

lay the little boy. Claire urged Nurse to explain that
they had come to inquire about the child's health and
that she was experienced in taking care of children.
The elderly nurse smiled grimly and spoke to the
woman. Then she turned to Claire and Mr. Bennett
and said, "It won't do no good tellin' her I like to take
care of little ones, Miss Claire, for she might think I
was trying to come over her, like. So I told her my gran
was a witch—may the good Lord forgive me—and
that I know some special cures. She'll like that som'at
better," she said apologetically to Mr. Bennett.

The rector smiled his appreciation. "You are an
admirably resourceful woman, Nurse Sutton. I can see
that you were indeed the best person to bring along.
Do you think that you could look at the child now and
see whether you think that he is very ill?"

With the mother's consent, the nurse approached
the child, talking to him in the same Anglo-Saxon dialect, which, it could be seen, put him at ease as it had
his mother. Claire and Mr. Bennett exchanged glances
that spoke much of the horror of these people's poverty before turning their attention back to the sick-bed.

After looking the boy over gently, all the while
conversing with the mother in a low voice, the nurse
turned towards them. "There's not so much wrong
with 'im that a load of food and a good scrubbin'
won't cure, sir," she reported, "but he isn't goin' to
get it 'ere. His mother don't 'ave it to give 'im, even if
she believed it would do 'im any good, which she
don't."

"It seems like their troubles started with that...that
big light thing that crossed the sky—you know the
one, more 'an five years back? Anyhow, she thinks it

was on account of it that her husband got pressed and her boy got snatched by a sweep to be a climbin' boy."

Mr. Bennett nodded grimly as he remembered. "The comet in 1811, I think it was. It was supposed to be a harbinger, wasn't it. Ask her how it was that he got away from the sweep," he requested.

After a minute Nurse answered, smiling, "It seems like this boy has some spunk, sir, 'cause he pretended to be stuck up in a chimbley one day and held on while they poked at 'im, until the sweep got fed up with waitin' an' loped off. Then before the folks there could get anybody to do anything about it, he scampered down and out the door and made it back home. And he's been here since, sir...that is until he went into the village and fell in the dust heap."

"Spunk, indeed," said the rector with sincere admiration on his face. Then, looking at Claire, he said, "It seems to me we should take him to my house and get him cleaned up and fed."

"I have a better suggestion," said Claire. "I am sure that Nurse would be more comfortable, and the boy's mother, too—surely you see that she cannot be left here, either—if they all came to my parents' house. You do not have the resources to care for them for long and I am convinced that it will be some time before this child can be considered healthy again."

Mr. Bennett had opened his mouth to protest but the logic of her argument stopped him. After a moment's hesitation he agreed.

"I am afraid that your parents will be shocked when they receive such a visit," was his only comment, though he sounded bitter.

"Nonsense," said Claire, not understanding his bitterness. "They are not so faint hearted, as you know."

His face cleared and he smiled. "No, they are not and neither are you." He looked at her for a long moment with something that went beyond admiration, and Claire felt herself flush with pleasure. Then, abruptly he turned and, requesting Nurse to explain their intentions to the boy's mother as best she could, he strode quickly out to the carriage to retrieve the blankets that Claire had brought, then returned and gently wrapped them around the child. In a few seconds he had the boy in his arms and was carrying him out to the carriage.

Claire was lost in admiration of the tenderness he had shown towards the boy. It was as if he had been carrying the most delicate flower. She came to her senses and hastened out to the carriage with Nurse and the boy's mother.

When they were installed in the back—the woman a bit frightened to find herself riding in a vehicle and the boy visibly delighted—Mr. Bennett handed Claire into the front, not meeting her gaze.

He was unusually silent for the first part of their trip back, but after some time he commented, "You see now why I was so eager to start some kind of village school. It is partially ignorance that keeps these people in their place, you know. All these lingering beliefs in omens, boggarts, witches, gabble ratchets and what have you—such notions only keep them from questioning their fate and doing something about their condition."

Claire agreed with him, but for a moment she could not answer. Finally she said, "No one should live like that."

"There was some evidence of poaching in the cottage," said the rector. "I suppose that was how they have been able to survive. It is a lucky thing for her that we came along before she was caught, or she would more than likely have been hanged."

Claire turned pale. "Surely not!" she exclaimed, but there was doubt in her voice. "Lord Sitchville would never do anything so horrible as to prosecute her."

"Wouldn't he?" asked the rector sardonically. "My cousin would." Then, remembering Claire's rumoured connection with Lord Babcock and seeing the horror in her face, he looked away. "Well, perhaps you know Lord Sitchville better than I," was all he said.

As they began to drive past the rectory, he again turned towards her and spoke. "I will come home with you and help carry the boy into the house."

"There is no need," she assured him. "One of the footmen can do that, and there will be such a bustle to find rooms for him and his mother and to get them both bathed, that you might find yourself in the way."

He laughed, relieving somewhat the grim look he had borne throughout their ride home. "You are probably right. I imagine there will be quite a commotion, for if the child has so much spunk, he will not give in easily. But I do not like to leave you with all of the work."

Claire laughed delightedly. "You need have no fear on that account," she replied. "I have no intention of getting involved with bathing this child. Becky will take good care of that. I will occupy myself with explaining the circumstances to my mother and with finding some employment for the boy's mother."

"Then I suppose you can handle all that without me," he acknowledged, "though I do seem to have burdened you with a problem of my own."

"Nonsense," said Claire. "I am doing this because I want to."

Mr. Bennett pulled up the carriage at the rectory and handed the reins to Claire before getting down. Then he turned to her and took her hand to say goodbye. He was so tall that he hardly needed to raise his head.

With his eyes looking deeply into hers, he said, "I know that you do. There is no one like you...." He did not finish, but merely smiled a farewell and released her hand, not looking at her again.

But as she drove away, he turned to watch her depart. It had taken Claire's mention of his "resources" to remind him of his position, and he must not forget what that was. But the more he was with her, the more he wanted to forget it, in spite of the things that he must do. The only way he could be resigned to his profession was to use it to accomplish the most good possible, however little that might be and however many enemies he might make.

Christopher Bennett knew that the Church was too tied to the ruling class to want to disturb the status quo, and though there were others like himself, they were few and far between. The only way the Church dealt with poverty was through charity; there was no real interest in changing the lot of the poor. To work within that structure was more than frustration. It was futility.

He would have to be free to anger and offend people, and it meant that he could not risk involving someone else who might be hurt.

He thought of Claire's defence of Lord Sitchville, and then he thought of Babcock.

"Damn!" said Mr. Bennett bitterly. "Damn!"

CHAPTER TEN

LORD BABCOCK was spending an uncomfortable evening under the watchful eye of his mama. His behaviour at the picnic had not gone unnoticed nor had the fact that the Olivers had left the rectory without being escorted to their carriage by the young viscount. This was so uncharacteristic of Babcock, heretofore totally predictable, that his mother was anxious.

Babcock had never shown so much interest in a female before, not even in Claire, and yet it was understood throughout the countryside that he and Claire would someday be wed. Lady Sitchville was not particularly devoted to Claire, but did find her birth and fortune appropriate for a future daughter-in-law. She had always commended the sense of responsibility that had led her son to select a lady of the county, especially since Claire had no brothers on which to depend.

Such entails were scandalous, thought Lady Sitchville. It would be a shame to see such an old barony pass out of the direct line. Lady Sally should have had a son, she added smugly to herself.

At dinner, she had been unable to refrain from commenting on her son's behaviour at the rectory.

"Cecil!" she emitted in her standard bark. "You did not appear well this morning." Familiar with her son's concern for his own health, she expected this to be sufficient opening for her inquiry.

For once, Babcock did not want attention called to himself. Startled by his mother's call to attention, he began to stammer a reply, then became irritated. "I was perfectly well, Mama," he grumbled. "I see no need for you to hover over me so. A touch of the sun perhaps, but soon over. A delightful tour of Garby church, I thought, this morning," he added, attempting to divert the conversation. "I certainly had not expected such graciousness from the parson."

Lady Sitchville could not have been more taken aback by her son's speech. Never had she known him to be offended by an inquiry after his health. It was evidence of a stronger emotion than pleasure in his own consequence. She allowed him to change the subject, but vowed to recall him to his obligations should he show signs of wavering. The Sitchville name should not be associated with gossip of any kind, and though he had yet to speak to Claire, the affair was too expected by all concerned to be abandoned. She was certain that Miss Oliver's shunning of gay society was due to her expectations of Babcock.

Lord Babcock was labouring under a strong emotion, it was true. It was nothing less than love at first sight. To have an ideal of womanhood, so prescribed that only a form was needed to fill it, rendered its discovery perfect and complete. Today Babcock had found his ideal.

Her face and her figure were perfect, her comportment refined. She walked with scarce a movement of her head; her steps were small and her movements delicate. That this was all due to the tightness of her corset and the confinement of her padding did not disturb Babcock. It was dictated by the rules of fashion, so it was right and it was proper.

It was not that he had not seen many women who approached his ideal, for London was full of young ladies who dressed this way and affected conforming behaviour. But Lydia had something special, as he perceived on their first exchange. She was so gratified to be noticed by him, so maidenly modest, so admiring! It was not surprising that Lydia should be modest, considering her mother's constant assertions that she must conceal her natural attributes and also considering her lack of fortune.

And her admiration for Lord Babcock was, like his for her, based upon form rather than substance. Babcock would never admit to himself that other maidens' admiration for him could be feigned, but subconsciously he registered that there was something unique about Lydia's.

He compared her to Claire and found her superior in every respect but one—her fortune. To Babcock, Claire's wealth and respectable lineage had been her two most attractive features, and to do him justice, the wealth had not mattered much to him. How should it when compared to the estate he would inherit someday? But family was important to him. Fortunately Robert Willoughby, though a scapegrace, was irreproachable when it came to lineage, so there was no need for worry there.

All of this speculation was quite pleasant, but Babcock, who never had been one to shirk his duty, realized that there was one big impediment—Claire. Though he had never spoken to her of marriage, he knew that his words and actions had implied a promise. He also knew that his parents expected the alliance. He began to regret his possessive behaviour; he must have got her hopes up! Despairingly, he thought that it was too late, but he refused to accept defeat so easily. He must endeavour to change everyone's perception of the case—but subtly at first in order to test the possibility of his success. Then, if things went well, he could show his preference more overtly. He felt hope rising in him. He was very much in love.

Lord Babcock's campaign, for such was its spirit, began the very next morning. When he set out on his morning calls, he headed, not in the direction of the Oliver house as had been his wont, but directly for the Willoughbys' cottage. He was armed with a legitimate excuse, for he intended to invite the Willoughbys to the great unveiling of the Sitchville manor; the Olivers, he knew, had already been invited by Lady Sitchville herself.

Much discussion had taken place at the Sitchvilles' dinner table about the most appropriate way to unveil their mansion. Lord Sitchville had voted for a grand ball to show it off in the grandest style. Lady Sitchville liked the idea of a ball, but she wanted their friends to see not only the great hall, but also the kitchens and the servants' quarters, which were designed in a way of which she was most proud, so she suggested a less formal affair. Babcock voted for both in quick succession and easily persuaded his parents, so it was decided that a breakfast be held the second week in June with a complete tour of the house and stables, and then a ball the following week.

Normally confident of a welcome reception, Babcock was nonetheless anxious about his call on the Willoughbys this morning. He wondered briefly if he could possibly be mistaken in his quick assessment of Lydia, but when he saw her peeking out from behind her mother, who answered the door, his doubts were put to rest. She was quite surprised, but obviously thrilled by his call. He responded with a glowing smile, and then confidently entered the house.

Sophia Willoughby was no less gratified than her daughter. She fluttered around Lord Babcock like a butterfly, exclaimed her pleasure over his visit and rattled aimlessly in an effort to entertain him, but eventually even she realized that he was not giving her much of his attention. She ushered him into the parlour, apologizing all the while for receiving him at the door herself.

"For I had just been going to stick my head out the front door to see if there was a need to take an extra wrap along on our walk," she explained. "You know how unpredictable the weather is this time of the year. A cool breeze may be coming in at the window, but the sun outside may be fearfully hot. I would not want Lydia to be overcome by the heat."

"No, indeed," exclaimed Babcock, sincerely sharing her concern.

Lydia blushed charmingly at the tone of his voice, and her mother could scarcely contain her delight.

"You must tell us how the manor is coming along, my lord. It is so exciting for us to hear of its progress."

"You must come see it for yourself," replied Babcock. "In fact you find me on a commission from my mama to beg you to do so." (This was not precisely true.) "We shall be having a breakfast on June the fourteenth at one o'clock and it will be a great pleasure for me to escort you on a tour of the house and stables."

Both ladies expressed their acceptance in raptures, and Babcock basked in their gratitude. He felt more than ever that these were the most agreeable people of his acquaintance, and the joy on Lydia's face made her more beautiful than ever.

The three of them talked pleasurably for some time, or rather, Babcock talked and Sophia and Lydia listened, before the viscount came to the realization that he had outstayed a normal morning call. He rose apologetically and reluctantly to his feet, but was gratified by their obvious regret that he was leaving. His own reluctance was mirrored in the wistfulness on Lydia's face. Never had he felt so pulled by a look. But society dictated the acceptable length of a morning call, and he must not go against it. He took leave of them and headed for home, floating on air.

Lydia and Sophia could not contain their joy over his call. It was so kind of Lord Babcock! What a perfect gentleman! They had not minded his staying such a long while; indeed, it was not even mentioned.

Lydia was almost beside herself. She was experiencing new emotions that confused and frightened her, and she sought reassurance from her mother.

"Mama, it was so kind of Lord Babcock to call on us, but wasn't it unusual? I mean, he was not wont to do so before today. And he has been so kind to me. What does it mean, Mama?" Lydia blushed with modesty and anxiety.

Sophia, who had been off in the clouds, was brought back to earth with a crash by this simple question. She could not help but notice the looks Babcock had bestowed on her daughter, and this, along with his actions of the day before, confirmed that he had been much taken with her. She had been happily speculating on something beyond her wildest dreams for her daughter. True, sometimes she had dreamed of an accidental meeting between Lydia and a royal duke, had even gone so far as to wish for a chance to throw her in one's way, but she had never really believed in the possibility. But this time she could read real admiration in a young man's eyes, and he a peer with his own fortune!

But what *did* it mean? Lord Babcock was understood to be promised to Claire, even if there had not been an announcement of an engagement. Claire was Lydia's own cousin. She had the birth and the fortune to make her the perfect match for Babcock, too. He had always shown his intentions openly. Why then was he visiting Lydia with such admiration in his eyes?

Sophia's blood ran cold. She looked at her beloved daughter, her innocent expression, and realized a possible answer. She must protect her daughter from any illicit alliance. She would hate to think it of Lord Babcock, as fine a young man as they thought him, but she had to admit to herself that it was a possibility. She pulled herself together for Lydia's sake and determined on strict vigilance without divulging her fears to her daughter. She must damp the child's hopes, though, as soon as possible.

"I would not refine too much upon it, my dear," she said hurriedly. "He is a polite young man, and as he said, he was simply on an errand for his mama. And we are, of course, part of Claire's family and perhaps as such he feels that he should get to know us better."

Lydia looked as though she had been dashed with cold water. "Oh," she said as her face fell. "Yes, that must be it. Of course." Without Babcock there, without the look that he had given her there in the room with her, she accepted her mother's reasoning. She had learned to accept her lot in life and her bleak prospects. The sadness she felt was something that she had learned not to indulge in a long time ago, but it was back now much stronger than before. She did not realize that it was because her heart had responded to the love in Babcock's eyes.

CHAPTER ELEVEN

MR. BENNETT called at the Olivers' manor several times the following week to see how the young boy was getting along. It was discovered that his name was Sam and his mother's was Ethel. By the end of the week, they were more or less settled in and Sam was recovering rapidly under the constant care of Nurse Sutton.

"She is really quite sensible with the sick," commented Claire on one of his visits.

"That is true now, my dear," said Lady Sally who was busy with her needlework in the corner of the drawing room. "But when you were younger, she placed too much faith in Culpepper's Herbal. That all changed when she nearly killed the upstairs parlourmaid with too large a dose. I had to put a stop to it, of course, and at first I did not think that she would ever forgive me. But she has forgotten it now. Or at least she pretends to have forgotten it," she said with a twinkle, looking over her eyeglasses at their visitor.

Mr. Bennett laughed appreciatively. His respect for the entire Oliver family had only increased with this latest episode, for they dealt with the arrival of these two desperate people with barely a ripple in their composure. At a time when ladies of fashion insisted their sedan chairs be carried into a foyer before they would allow the curtains to be opened for fear of taking ill from the night air, they had shown no concern for their own health.

The child was not infectious, Claire's mother had said, and there was no reason at all to be concerned. They would find the pair a cottage on their own property and ascertain from the servants how they might best be employed.

"Have you found any place that Ethel might be able to work?" asked the rector. "For if you haven't, I might try to find a position. I fear, though, that she is not trained in any domestic work."

"That she isn't," confirmed Lady Sally, smiling. "But do not tax yourself. She will be able to work for a while as a kitchen maid. They have assured me in the kitchen that the extra pair of hands will be welcome, and there will be very little that she cannot learn rapidly there. Besides, Cook can understand her and the poor woman will be happier if she can improve her English gradually, you know. She will have enough changes to get used to as it is."

"I cannot thank you enough for undertaking this problem," said Mr. Bennett sincerely, but he was cut off by Lady Sally.

"Pooh!" she said. "It caused me no effort at all, as you well know. It was quite amusing for us all to hear the screams coming from the nursery when they were both bathed. I had not heard anything like it since Claire was little."

Claire spoke up with a start and coloured rapidly. "Mama! How can you tell such a horrid story! There is not a word of truth in it!"

"No, of course there isn't," said Lady Sally soothingly. "You must forgive me, Mr. Bennett, for treating you like one of the family. That was quite an improper thing for me to say in front of you. I was merely trying to see if Claire was awake, for she did not seem to be attending, but it was most improper."

Mr. Bennett had been doing his best not to laugh out loud, but he could not suppress a smile. "Your apology is accepted, my lady. I will take it as a compliment that you forgot your formality in my presence."

"Formality!" exclaimed Claire. "When could you possibly accuse my mama of too much formality? Or any formality, for that matter?" She had been embarrassed more by her mother's calling attention to her absent-mindedness than by her words, for her thoughts had been rather private. She had been thinking that Mr. Bennett seemed more withdrawn from her than he had been before their expedition to rescue Sam.

He had assumed a distance from her which was both respectful and proper, but there was something about it which she did not understand. Perhaps he had been offended by some comment that she had made, though he did not seem in the least angry. There was still a look in his eye that bespoke a good understanding between them, but there was much less openness. She had come to enjoy being a part of his many projects, even if only as a listener, and the distance he was putting between them seemed to exclude her from his confidence.

She could sit and enjoy the banter between her mother and the rector, but he made no effort to draw her in as he had been wont to do. She could be a part of his discussions with her father, but Mr. Bennett no longer looked her in the eye when he spoke. And yet, at times, Claire was sure that he watched her when she was not regarding him directly. It was both puzzling and distressing.

The next week, there was a bustle of activity which the county had not seen in some time. It was the week that everyone had looked forward to. It was the unveiling of the Sitchville mansion.

Mr. Bennett found himself on June the fourteenth on the way to the breakfast at Sitchville Park. He was not in a sunny humour. He had seen the necessity for putting a stop to the growing intimacy he was developing with Miss Oliver, but he was finding it very hard to bear up. He had not realized until he tried to do without it that her closeness had become so important to him.

He had continued to see her frequently, not by design, but by habit. Her whole family had entered into his projects so thoroughly that it was impossible to draw back from them without causing offence where he would least want to do so. His friendship with her parents could continue much as before, but their acceptance of him into their family circle only made the distance he had placed between Claire and himself harder to maintain. He wished that he had not got so close to her before he saw the danger to his own heart, but he could grimly comfort himself with the knowledge that nothing in her demeanour suggested that she had been similarly affected. Mr. Bennett, who could usually see the humour in any situation, was finding it more and more difficult to see it in this one.

Claire had been trying to distract herself with preparations for the Sitchvilles' breakfast party and ball, but she was preoccupied with thoughts about the rector. She no longer thought that she had done something to offend him, for many reasons. There was his happy reception of her and her father in his library on their last visit. His face had lit up when he saw her, almost involuntarily, and she had responded with a smile, but no sooner were they welcomed than his restraint returned. She thought about the several times that he had appeared to have some private concern before she had come to know him better. That had disappeared for a while from his manner, but now it was present again. The strange thing was that whatever was troubling him did not affect his friendship with her parents, just with herself. She could not dismiss it as mere moodiness.

Claire now saw how much his friendship and companionship had come to mean to her. Seeing him was the greatest joy in her life, for there had never been another person with whom she could talk as she talked to him. It was an unusual friendship, she knew, which could transcend the barriers of social position and gender. There was nothing wrong in that, she told herself, but she was afraid to look any closer at the implications. She thought herself free of social considerations that she deemed not worthy of notice.

There was one possibility which she could scarcely credit, except that much of the gossip seemed to support it. Perhaps he was thinking of marrying; everyone seemed to think it part of his duty. Might he not be considering making a proposal? Might it be to Lydia? It was unthinkable in many ways, but Claire could see how it would make him shrink from friendship with another woman. And it would not likely be something which he would discuss with her. She knew that her aunt was doing everything in her power to put Lydia in his company as often as possible.

On the appointed day, Claire and her parents arrived at Sitchville Park within a few minutes of one o'clock. They had breakfasted at their own home on the sly, fearing the fashionable nature of Lady Sitchville's "breakfast" might lead her to withhold food from the guests until three in the afternoon. They came with a great deal of curiosity and no small measure of amusement at what they were about to see.

As they entered the grounds, they passed a new gatehouse with Gothic influences and drove under a Gothic arch. And when the main house came into view, Lord Oliver said dryly, "Sally, my darling, it looks as though Sophia has been vindicated."

There, as she had promised, were the moat, the battlements and the drawbridge. The moat did not surround the house and was too far from it to serve as a dry moat for lighting the servants' quarters. Instead it was filled with water, from what source they did not know, and it curved gently from one front corner of the house to another to pass under the drawbridge. The drawbridge served only to cross the moat, and the coachman negotiated it up to the front of the house.

The house had acquired an imposing new façade of flat stone with Gothic arches and massive oak doors at intervals. The roof was squared off with battlements and turrets at three of the corners. From what they could see, the right side of the house extended for many yards with smaller arches repeated at intervals, but the left side ended at the main section with the common rooms.

The coachman drove their carriage up to where the front door of the house had been and found an imposing Gothic portico in its place. They alighted under the massive colonnade and proceeded through the doorway into a sort of vestibule that opened into the great hall.

Lady Sitchville was positioned near the door to the vestibule to receive her guests. It was evident to the Olivers that there was already a large number assembled which represented a house party, perhaps twenty guests in all. Undoubtedly it was the first of many house parties planned to show off the new house to the Sitchvilles' town friends, but these people would be staying on for the ball the following week.

Lady Sitchville was radiant with pride when she greeted the Olivers. "Justin, Sally, Claire—what a pleasure to see you," she began. "What do you think of the hall? You must tell me at once."

Lady Sally groped for words, but inspiration came to her, "It is splendid, Theresa. We are overcome. It is . . . reminiscent of one's noblest ancestors," she concluded, borrowing from her sister-in-law.

Claire heard her father murmur, "Yes, but whose ancestors?" She tried not to laugh, and managed a reasonably sincere expression of admiration.

The Olivers looked around them at the formidable room. It was panelled on three sides in heavy oak and had enormous beams in the ceiling. At one end was a dais on which sat an imposing oak table, with chairs placed behind it so that everyone seated there would be facing the hall. It was clearly a copy of the baronial hall of old. Coats of arms were carved in the panels, and suits of armour were posted like sentries at the main doors.

In spite of these forbidding items, the room was furnished for the day with delicate tables and chairs, arranged for the upcoming breakfast, in the most modern fashion. The upholstery was of the finest silk, flowers adorned each table, and the tablecloths were hemmed with lace. The contrast of the furnishings was no more astonishing than the contrast of the fourth wall, which was also the back wall of the house. It was covered with large plates of glass, which allowed one to look out over the gardens. Double doors, also of glass, opened to permit the guests to stroll in and out.

When Lady Sitchville left the Olivers' side to welcome more guests, they were joined by Mr. Bennett. He had seen them enter and had waited only for them to be greeted to approach them. Lord Oliver and Lady Sally received him with their customary pleasure, but Claire, though pleased to see him, merely smiled. The rector addressed his remarks to Claire's father, but his eyes avoided Claire's with difficulty.

"Dare I ask you, Lord Oliver, your impressions of the renovations?" he asked, barely suppressing a smile.

Claire's father was sympathetic enough with the rector's sentiments to answer sincerely, "When I heard that Sitch had fortified his manor, it alarmed me. I was not sure that I was up to mounting an attack on a well-fortified castle at my age. But now that I see the back side of the house, I am comforted that I will be able to manage it."

Mr. Bennett smiled in appreciation. "You don't have any plans yourself for a 'castellation' of the Oliver manor?"

"No," said the baron in mock seriousness. "As I explained to you before, I am getting too old for anything so adventurous. But perhaps Robert would be interested in some such thing for the cottage. I'll have to ask him."

Claire and her mother joined in the laughter over this, but they had to stop when Lord Babcock joined them. It was time to be seated for breakfast, and he had come to lead Claire to his table. As Claire accepted his arm, she could feel Mr. Bennett's eyes following them. In place of the embarrassment she had felt on similar occasions, there was only a heaviness in her heart.

Babcock led her to the table where an elaborate array of foods had been laid out. She had her choice of hot or cold breads, white or dark, cold meats of all kinds, honey and cakes, and chocolate to drink, before being led to the dais at the end of the room and seated at the principal table.

It was not many minutes before Claire noticed a difference in Babcock's manner towards her. He was polite as usual, but there were none of the meaningful looks, the fulsome compliments, and the lingering touches of her hand that she had grown to anticipate with such distaste. She might have been any distant acquaintance, except for the necessary assumption which had brought him to her side. It was a welcome change and made her think that she just might enjoy the afternoon before her, but she was curious all the same. If Babcock was going to change the behaviour he had exhibited towards her for almost five years now, there must be good reason for it.

His lack of attention, however, allowed her mind to drift in the direction it was pulling her. She had seen Mr. Bennett seat himself in front of her, choosing the chair that faced her directly. He was making polite conversation with the young lady on his right, but occasionally he lifted his eyes to look at Claire. She felt very awkward at those moments to be caught watching him, and yet she found it difficult to keep her eyes averted from that spot. It was, she told herself, because he was straight in front of her that the difficulty existed.

She turned abruptly towards Babcock after one of these moments and launched into a new conversation, trying to take her mind off the incident.

"Tell me, Lord Babcock, have you yet had the chance to be presented to my cousin Lydia?"

Claire was astonished at the reaction to this random attempt at conversation. Babcock seemed to gasp, which caused him to choke on the piece of food that was in his mouth. At the same instant, he looked sideways at her with alarm. It took many minutes before his coughing subsided, during which time he became quite red in the face. When he was finally able to regain some of his composure, he said in a croaking voice, with still a touch of alarm in his eyes, "What was it that you asked me, Miss Oliver?"

Almost afraid to set him off again, Claire replied carefully, "It was merely a passing thought. I wondered if you had had an opportunity to meet my cousin, Lydia Willoughby. She was not 'out' when you were home last, I believe."

The alarm in Babcock's eyes receded slowly and he answered with an air of nonchalance. "Yes, I believe I have had the pleasure. Your Aunt and Uncle Willoughby's daughter, is she not? We have not had much occasion to speak, though," he added hastily.

Claire had been absorbed in her own affairs, but Babcock's manner was strange enough to alert her to something. She began to wonder if she had not stumbled across the answer to his change towards herself. She watched Babcock throw a furtive glance at a corner of the room, saw that Lydia was seated there, and knew that he had long been aware of it.

"She is charming, isn't she?" Claire asked innocently.

Babcock stumbled over his words in replying, "Yes, certainly...that is, I hadn't noticed particularly...although naturally she would be, being your cousin." He smiled as though pleased with his answer.

"She is by nature a very sweet girl," Claire continued. "She is very devoted to her mama and to projects of an improving nature. At the same time, you can see that she is quite fashionable and very lovely." As Claire continued to describe Lydia in this complimentary fashion, she was amused to notice the changes in Babcock's expression. He began with a studied air of indifference, but as his eyes necessarily rested on Lydia, he seemed unable to school his features, and a lost, rather dreaming look came over them. When Claire stopped speaking, he did not appear to notice.

She took advantage of the fact to turn her notice back to the room at large, a broad smile on her face.

Mr. Bennett had been observing Claire and Babcock in conversation, obviously in agreement with one another. He was too absorbed by his own feelings to notice the direction of Babcock's gaze, and only saw the pleasure on Claire's face. He tried to conceal the frustration and anger that mounted in him by turning to the guest on his right, but he alarmed that young lady nonetheless by the heavy frown on his brow.

Claire caught the movement of his head as she turned, but was not certain that he had been looking in her direction. The sight of him caused the smile on her face to disappear and the feeling of heaviness to descend on her chest again. She shook herself reproachfully and told herself that she was behaving foolishly, but to little avail.

Shortly thereafter, Lady Sitchville signalled to her steward, who then moved to speak to several of the guests, mostly the local contingency, while she herself rose from her seat to join this eager group at one of the side doors of the hall to begin the tour. The house guests, who had already had a chance to see the renovations, were left to their own amusements. Lord Babcock turned to Claire and said that he would be happy to be her escort on the tour. Claire would have preferred to walk with her father so as not to miss his caustic comments, but it could not be helped. She resigned herself to waiting until she and her parents were home once again before hearing them.

As she and Lord Babcock joined Lady Sitchville, a small parade of other guests formed behind them. Lydia and her mother approached the group at the same time as Mr. Bennett, and so the rector offered an arm to each lady and placed himself directly behind

Claire and Babcock. He would have been quite surprised to know how uncomfortable they were both rendered by this act.

"I am happy to see you all here today," began Lady Sitchville importantly. "You are very kind to show an interest in our house. I will not take you all over it, of course, but we will see as much as you would like. And perhaps the young people will continue on to the stables afterwards to see the changes there. My son can take you, but it would be too much for all of us, I think. Now. Let us start with the drawing room."

She led them into a feminine-looking room of which she was obviously proud. The furniture was delicate and made of rosewood with silk and chintz upholstery. Large mirrors in gilt frames covered the walls. As was the entire manor, the room was lit by enormous oil lamps, hung from the ceiling. Lady Sitchville pointed out the evidence of hot-air heating, never before seen in the county, which had been installed throughout the house.

"The one exception will be in my rooms and Lord Sitchville's, where we have put in a type of steam heating," she explained. "We wanted to try it, but we felt it was simply too new an invention to risk putting throughout the house. Though I do know," she added as an afterthought, "that the Prince Regent has used it in the kitchens at Brighton." There was a general hum of admiration.

She then led them into the dining room, which was off the great hall. It was very masculine in character, with heavy carved wood panelling and massive mahogany furniture. Rich Turkish carpets covered the floor. The furniture had an air of permanence, and the profuse use of English oak on the walls conveyed the same sense of strength and stability as the three panelled walls of the great hall.

There was a serving room off the dining room where the food could be kept heated after its long trek from the kitchens. From there a dark passage snaked its way back to the servants' quarters, but Lady Sitchville avoided this and ushered her guests toward the conservatory, which seemed designed to hide the servants' wing from the rest of the house. Located at the back corner of the main section of the house, it protruded far from the body of the house and seemed to be made entirely of large plates of glass.

Claire recalled that the library of the old manor, which had always interested her father, had been in the part of the house now completely taken up by the great hall. The same thought must have been in her father's mind, for when they had finished seeing the common rooms on the right side of the house he asked about it.

"Oh, yes," answered Lady Sitchville in a dismissive tone, "the library. Well, as rooms go, I suppose it was very nice in its way, but we decided the space could be better devoted to the hall. We will have writing tables in it and the billiard table, and use it in that way when we are not entertaining. Sitchville, of course, has his study on the other side of the hall, with his own bath and water closet. You will think it strange," she added with a titter of laughter, "but I must show you the water closet. It has been so cleverly hidden in a cupboard behind the wood panelling. One would never know it was there."

The entire party crossed the great hall once more and entered Lord Sitchville's set of apartments. The masculine character of the dining room was repeated here, with oak panelling and heavily carved desk, chairs and bookcases. The books that the Olivers remembered were not in evidence, however, and the room seemed fitted only as a morning room for the gentlemen and for Lord Sitchville's estate business.

Lord Oliver was irritated, and he turned to speak to his wife in a low tone.

"I wonder if I dare ask what has become of the books. I would like to acquire them if they haven't been thrown out as jettison. Do you think that I would be thought a bit out of date?"

Lady Sally only smiled wryly at him and patted his hand.

Lady Sitchville, meanwhile, was guiding the group into her husband's other rooms, showing them the water closet, so carefully hidden, and his bath, with gilded washstand, dressing stand, gilded basin and ewers.

"My apartments are just above," she explained proudly. "The water is pumped directly upstairs from here to my bath and the housemaids' closet. The hot and cold water are separate. My bath is off my dressing room, of course, and is similarly decorated. My husband, as you can see, decided to install a shower-bath for himself."

As if finished with the tour, she began to lead everyone back to the hall, only to be stopped by Lady Sally. "Theresa," she asked, "you might not care to show us, but I declare that I am very curious to see the kitchens and the servants' quarters. Would you mind?"

Lady Sitchville feigned uncertainty at first, as if the proposal made her uncomfortable, but in fact she was extremely proud of the quarters. She simply did not want to make a display of this pride to her guests. Modesty, after all, was a virtue. So, keeping up her pretence, she agreed to Lady Oliver's request with an air of daring. The group traipsed back across the hall and entered the dark corridor to the kitchens. Claire could hear behind her the affected tittering of the ladies, who were acting as though a visit to the servants' quarters was a bit shocking, even though all of these women had houses much smaller, where servants were stationed in the entrance hall and the mistress made daily trips to the kitchen. Hearing her Aunt Sophia's laugh among them, she wondered what Mr. Bennett was thinking of it all.

The many turns and twists in the hall, purposely created to prevent odours from the kitchen from reaching the main part of the house, were carefully negotiated by the ladies in their long skirts. The first set of rooms they came to were the steward's room and its satellites: the butler's pantry with the plate storage safe, the scullery, the wine cellars and cells for brushing clothes, cleaning shoes, polishing knives, and trimming, cleaning and filling oil lamps. The steward's room was enormous, providing as it did the dining room for the steward, the housekeeper, the head cook, head gardener, senior ladies' maids, valets, coachman and visiting servants in a house that routinely employed more than forty indoor servants.

A staircase rose steeply from this part of the wing. Lady Sitchville mentioned significantly that this led to the male servants' dormitory.

The group then passed into the main servants' hall where the lower-echelon servants ate their meals. Located here also were the bells, labelled for each room in the house, so that servants could remain in their quarters and yet respond quickly to the masters' requests. This provided a privacy from the servants that smaller houses did not have, and many of the guests regarded it enviously. The kitchen lay beyond, along with the housekeeper's room and its satellites, rooms for housekeeping functions performed by female servants.

A separate staircase led from the kitchen up to the female servants' dormitory. Lady Sitchville explained quite proudly and self-righteously, "The servants' wing has been designed to keep the male and female servants apart as much as possible, and with these staircases, the only time they need be in the same room is when they have their meals."

Claire cringed on hearing this speech, and behind her she heard Mr. Bennett clear his throat. She darted a look at the footman who had accompanied the group to open doors for them, but his face was impassive. No doubt he was used to being embarrassed, being a part of this household, but she wondered how he felt about being discussed in such a way.

The farthermost part of the house, which gave access to the yards, was not explored. When asked about it, Lady Sitchville dismissed it as the laundry and of little interest, so they all turned back and made their way once again to the great hall. Here, Lady Sitchville suggested to the older guests that they remain with her, and to the younger that they follow Lord Babcock outside to see the stables.

Claire would rather have remained inside at this point, but unsure how to suggest it, she walked through the double glass doors on Babcock's arm. As Sophia stayed behind with the others, Lydia was left to accept Mr. Bennett's lone escort, and the pair followed closely on Claire's and Babcock's heels.

Claire and Babcock passed the time discussing the changes to the house, though both were uncomfortably aware of the implications of such a topic. It became a strained conversation, with Claire taking pains to show no more than polite interest and Babcock trying to make it clear by his tone of voice that Claire's opinion of the manor was of little interest to him.

Behind them, Mr. Bennett and Lydia were silent. The rector found it difficult to converse with Lydia at the best of times, but even the subject of the house did not draw her out today, though she was clearly impressed. After a few futile attempts, he gave up and instead followed the conversation in front of him, not liking the sound of it, for he missed the overtones.

The stables were soon reached, and they saw that the Gothic-castle theme had been repeated, though to a lesser extent. There were more Gothic arches for doorways, and the same stone was used, but inside it was much like any other large stable. They continued in to see Sarravano, the pride of the Sitchvilles' stable, their hope to win the Derby.

Stationed at the horse's head was a small, sharp-featured man with eyes that darted about quickly as he bowed his head respectfully to Lord Babcock. Claire identified him as Tucker, the trainer who had so impressed her Uncle Robert, and she took a rare and instant dislike to him. There was something about the way his eyes seemed to be constantly shifting—especially when Babcock was not observing him—that she found dishonest and repugnant. She suddenly felt anxious about this man's influence over her uncle.

Lord Babcock proudly presented his horse to the assembly, "Ladies and gentlemen, the next winner of the Derby!"

"What about that colt of Sir George's?" asked one of the guests. "Won't he present a problem?"

Babcock brushed this aside confidently. "Magnifico may be a fine horse," he granted, "but he does not pose a challenge to this one."

"How do they bet their money at Tattersall's?" asked another.

"I have been assured," replied Babcock, "that it goes heavily in our favour."

After a little more in this vein, the viscount moved on to discuss the points of yet another colt with one of his guests. When the young people had entered the stables, they had dropped their two-by-two formation to wander about singly and look at the various horses, forming and unforming groups casually as they strolled. Mr. Bennett had gravitated unconsciously toward Claire, who was chatting with other guests, though with no one in particular.

Lydia, left to herself, wandered near Sarravano, trying to see what was so special about the animal and knowing there must be something because *he* had said so. She was not comfortable around horses, not knowing how to ride, but she wanted to show an interest.

Tucker was still at the horse's head. He knew this young lady was Robert Willoughby's daughter because he had seen them out together one day, but Lydia was quite unaware of the amount of time her father spent with Tucker in the stable. The trainer had little respect for Robert, thinking him a gullible fool, and his disrespect overflowed into his behaviour with Lydia. He knew that he had nothing to fear from her father.

"Coo there, miss," he said to her with a leer, speaking in a thieves' cant she would not recognize. "You're that Miss Willoughby now, aren't you? You're a swell mort, you are. As fine a bit o' blood an' bone as this here horse. Why don't you come along o' here one o' these days and I'll give you a ride on 'im— for a coachwheel I will."

Lydia was frightened. She had approached the horse fearfully, so her heartbeat was already elevated. And now this strange man was speaking to her with words she did not understand. But she did understand the leer, though she could not imagine his reason for singling her out. Her fear increased, and she was paralysed into inaction. She knew she ought to seek out Mr. Bennett, but she was mesmerized by Tucker's ogling stare. Lydia's figure had drawn men's gazes before, but never with this degree of disrespect, and the proximity of the horse, the unfamiliar smell of the stables, and the crowd all had their effect.

Her heart beat even faster, and Tucker's face, with the leer that seemed to become more and more ghastly as he continued to talk, began to waver in front of her eyes. After a series of gasps to get more air than her corset would permit, she fainted dead away.

Lord Babcock, who had been keeping a secretive eye on Lydia from across the stables, gave a startled yelp and leaped to her side. He knelt and began to chafe her hands as he implored her to come to.

Tucker, who had been truly alarmed by Lydia's faint, was babbling in defence of himself, "I didn't do nothing to th' mort—er, the lady—my lord! Really I didn't. The lady just fainted away. I swear it!"

Babcock responded impatiently, "No one's blaming you, you fool. Run up to the house and get some assistance. Tell them Miss Willoughby's fainted. Better yet, tell them I am bringing her up to the house. We will need some brandy in the drawing room."

Mr. Bennett had stepped up only moments after Babcock and was in time to hear Tucker's expostulations. He was of the mind that anyone who protested his innocence to that extent had a reason to fear being blamed, and he stared intently at Tucker. He saw the relieved and cunning smile that crossed the man's face when Babcock dismissed him. And looking up as he started for the house, Tucker noticed the rector's watchful eyes. Assuming a look of polite deference, he departed hastily.

Claire was at first quite worried about her cousin and wanted to send immediately for her mother, but soon Lydia began to come round. She moaned gently. Then, when Babcock asked her if she was all right, she tried to rise, apologizing to him.

"Oh, my lord, I am so sorry," she said weakly, plainly embarrassed. "I cannot think what came over me. I was just looking at your beautiful horse and..." Suddenly she remembered Tucker and she looked around fearfully. The remembrance caused her to fall back onto Babcock's supporting arm.

"Please do not try to rise, my dear Miss Willoughby," he begged. "I will see what I can do to get you to the house, if you will permit me." And with that, in spite of her feeble protests, he gently lifted her up in his arms.

Mr. Bennett spoke up quickly. "I will escort Miss Oliver and the others back to the house," he offered.

"What? Oh, yes, of course," recalled Babcock, who was experiencing a delicious feeling of mastery with Lydia in his arms. "Much obliged." And barely acknowledging Claire as he passed, he headed toward the house with the treasured bundle held close to his chest.

The other guests, observing Lord Babcock's departure, began to drift back in the direction of the house on their own. Claire watched them go for a moment and then turned to take Mr. Bennett's arm. They found themselves following the others back to the house, almost alone in each other's company.

Mr. Bennett was quite content for it to be so. He was finding it a strain to be constantly protecting himself from spending too much time with Claire and the prospect of this time with her, even for so short a walk, was bliss. He allowed himself to relax and forget about all else for the moment.

Claire's heart quickened at the prospect of talking to him alone. They had not had such an occasion since the picnic at the rectory, and she feared that the constraint which he had recently shown around her might make the time pass awkwardly. But looking up, she saw his relaxed features, and she knew that for some reason the constraint was gone. Then she smiled so sweetly at him that it almost took his breath away.

"Lord Babcock seems to have handled that quite well," began Mr. Bennett, not knowing, now that he finally had her to himself, quite how to begin. "Quite masterfully, in fact."

Claire gave a small secretive smile which he found hard to interpret. "Yes, he did," she agreed.

After a minute's silence, he began again. "What did you think of Lady Sitchville's tour of the manor?" he asked with the humorous smile she found so hard to resist.

She laughed lightly, not sure just how candid to be. "Well, let me say that it was quite like Lady Sitchville," she began.

"That it was," he said wryly. "The house speaks for them very well. The air of authority of the house's façade is quite threatening, wouldn't you say? It lets one know that the aristocratic defences are up. And the lavishness, right down to the water closets, obscures the black source of the money. Except the servants' closets, I suppose. I imagine they are still dank earthen holes out back."

Claire did not comment, but it was clear she was in agreement with him. "I was distressed to hear her refer to the servants in such a demeaning way, especially in front of one of them. I wondered how he felt, but his face gave nothing away."

"Of course not. He would have been turned out if it had. Don't distress yourself over it. In all probability, he believes Lady Sitchville has every right to talk about him in that way. He was raised for domestic service and it is unlikely that he questions her rights over him. It was rather amusing, though, the way in which Lady Sitchville dismissed the laundry. It is, of course, the Achilles heel of the perfectly moral house.''

"What do you mean?" asked Claire, genuinely puzzled.

He smiled down at her. "Why, don't you know? That is the one place where she cannot prevent the male and female servants from seeing one another. The laundry has to be outside, which puts it near the stables, and the laundry maids and the grooms can see each other without much fear of being caught. Have you never noticed that the prettiest serving girls choose to work in the laundry?"

Claire felt herself blush. The heat rose from somewhere deep inside her all the way to her cheeks. Why was it, she thought, that she was so missish with this man? She had frequently "pooh-poohed" Babcock's sense of delicacy, but any time Mr. Bennett mentioned something that bordered on the intimate she became quite unsettled. Venturing a look at his face, she saw that he was aware of her embarrassment and was amused by it.

"Well, I see that we are nearing the house," she said briskly to change the subject, and she stepped up her pace.

His hand held her back.

"Wait just a moment, Miss Oliver," he said, reluctant to let her go. "There cannot be any reason to hurry. I think your cousin is in good hands."

Claire's heart quickened at the tone of his voice. She turned to face him, sensing his need to be with her and knowing that it was what she wanted, too. As she looked up at him, Mr. Bennett read something in her eyes that made him draw in his breath sharply. He seemed about to speak, but checked himself and turned away, releasing her arm. For a moment he said nothing, and Claire could feel the struggle that was going on inside him, even though she did not understand what it was.

When he did speak, it was on a subject that surprised her.

"I seem to remember, Miss Oliver, that when we first met I explained to you that I had entered the Church with some reluctance." He looked back at her as if to see whether she remembered it, as well.

"Yes, you did," Claire confirmed. "You said it was your cousin's wish, but that you'd had other ideas." She was quite puzzled now and wanted him to go on.

"I do not think that I ever explained what it was that finally persuaded me to give in to his wishes," he said, once again making her feel a distance between them which she did not understand. "I have wanted you to know that I did not just give in because I was unable to have my own way." Knowing him as she now did, Claire did not think anything of the kind, so she smiled at him, which he did not see, having turned his face away.

He continued, "After running through all the possible livings I could possibly have wanted—and I assure you that there were many besides those I told you about—there was not much else that I could do." He kept his eyes diverted from her face and gazed back toward the manor, but she could tell that he was determined that she understand his explanations.

"I could never had lived totally as a man of leisure," he said, "even if my cousin had been willing to support me, which of course he was not. Call it *noblesse oblige*, if you will, but I do feel the need to do something useful. At any rate, I resisted going into the Church because it seemed such a damned parasitical life.

"I had only been exposed to Twickenhams, too, you see," he continued, "until one day I met someone different. It was a fellow by the name of Charles James Blomfield—I don't know if you have heard of him. Anyway, he was something of a pariah among his clerical associates because he was quite the classical scholar and strongly supported Catholic Emancipation. You can imagine how they regarded him.

"Then, when I returned from that unpleasant experience in America, I heard about another parson by the name of Daniel Wilson, who was at St. John's Chapel in Bedford Row. And it was seeing him that finally made me realize that I could enter the Church without comprising myself, strange as that may sound.

"That man, by the sheer strength of his personality and his integrity, was able to attract a large number of merchants and lawyers from that particular part of London to his services regularly to hear what he had to say, and to persuade them that there were more important things in their lives than material possessions. That is a difficult group to convince of that, as you can imagine."

Claire was watching the rector intently but expectantly, as if waiting for him to explain just why he thought it necessary to tell her all this. He took a deep breath before continuing.

"So you see, it was meeting those two men that convinced me that I could go into the Church without giving up some of the goals I had set out for myself. I did not, and I do not, foresee that I will be able to accomplish as much as I could if I were in Parliament, for example, but at least I can carry out some course of action. My cousin did not have the sense to see that I would do it this way, fortunately, or he never would have used his influence to get me this preferment. Do you understand what I am saying?'' he asked her, suddenly turning towards her.

"Yes," Claire said, but with reservation in her tone. She knew that he was not asking if she had understood his words only, for he had never doubted her understanding before. There was more to come, and he was just asking her if she had followed him thus far before going on.

Mr. Bennett looked at her intently. His expression was inscrutable, but she was reminded of the first impression she had had of him, a time that now seemed so long ago. Then she had sensed a care in him, perhaps a disappointment or a reason for discontent. Now that feeling was intensified, and she knew that he was bitterly unhappy, perhaps felt hopeless, though his control was undiminished. And her heartbeat quickened as she realized that whatever he had yet to say had something to do with her and was the reason he was telling her this.

Mr. Bennett did have more to say, and he knew that there would not likely be another chance to talk to Claire alone, but just as he was about to go on, he saw Lady Sally coming out into the grounds.

"Your mother is coming to take you home, I think," he said, taking a deep breath. Then, for a brief moment, he took her hand, looking at her slim fingers lying in his own, and released it. And in a voice totally empty of emotion he said, "I shouldn't wonder if Lord Babcock has not sent her to find you."

Claire started as if she had been rudely awakened from a dream. His gesture in taking her hand, the gentleness of his touch, had moved her, and his mention of Lord Babcock in connection with herself was as unexpected as a note played out of tune. As her mother approached, she searched his face for some indication of his meaning, but it was as if he had pulled down a screen between them. The only thing she saw on his face was a trace of unhappiness. It was really only something she sensed more than saw, yet knowing him as she did, she felt sure it was there.

Lady Sally by this time had reached them, and they both greeted her with schooled smiles.

"Such a hoop-la, my dears," were her first words. "Lydia has been brought to the house in faints. But I forget, you were probably with them. Well, I do not wonder at your avoiding the ensuing scenes, but all is well now. The only thing is that Sophia requests our carriage to carry her back home, and your father thinks that we might as well go on ourselves. Babcock is quite anxious to see her off, too; he must fear another episode. You know his own health is so, er, precarious that I think he sympathizes with her sincerely."

All of this was related at Lady Sally's normal speedy rate as they walked back to the manor, and in no time they had made their goodbyes to Lord and Lady Sitchville. Claire noted that Mr. Bennett fell back on their way through the hall, so that by the time they reached the vestibule he was no longer with their party. Lord Babcock was on hand to help them into their carriage, but from the rector, there was no goodbye at all.

CHAPTER TWELVE

CLAIRE RETURNED HOME in a most unsettled state of mind. Mr. Bennett's words to her had been prematurely ended, of that she was sure, and yet he had made no attempt to engage her at some future date so that he could finish them. It was as if he did not want to distinguish them with too much importance, though her instincts told her that what he had left to say would be of great significance to them both.

She sought for clues in the things he had already said, but they did not lead her to any conclusions. She already knew him for a highly principled man, a reformer, almost a radical. And, she thought, it was not really necessary for him to make her see that he was determined to be different from the run-of-the-mill clergyman; that was obvious in his every act. He did not need to explain to her the state of the English clergy, nor even that there were a few men, like himself, who were prepared to go against the grain and work for the common good. So why had he done it?

That night Claire slept poorly, unable to shake off her conviction that Mr. Bennett's words had been only a preamble to something more. His behaviour over the past week had worried her already, so that she had thought of little else, and now, in spite of her attempts to put it aside, her worry intensified. She wondered if he had not chosen some new course of action—his manner suggested that—and she feared that it might involve his going away. Try as she might, Claire was unable to rest comfortably when this fear kept recurring in her mind.

In the morning she was calmer, but when she thought of his last words to her, she experienced the same jolt she had felt when he had mentioned Babcock's name as their conversation was interrupted the day before. Mr. Bennett was the one person who had never made references to her supposed relationship with Babcock. It would have been most improper of him to do so, but at the same time Claire had been comforted to have this one friend, so dear to her, who had seemed to have no preconceived notions about her.

And then he had mentioned Babcock in a way that had chilled her. For the first time there had been a suggestion in his tone, an innuendo in his words. For her, though, it had been like a statement of fact—and one that for some reason made her feel as though her fate had been sealed.

Claire knew that she had to speak to Mr. Bennett privately again; she had to know more of what he'd wanted to say to her. The easiest way to accomplish that would be to call on him with her father with the excuse of coming for more books and then to suggest a turn around the garden. She knew that she would be able to do it naturally and also that her father would not join them.

Claire dressed hurriedly and went down to breakfast, hoping to catch her father in the dining room. But it was evident that he had already breakfasted and gone out to see his bailiff. She ate very little, alone, waiting for him to return to the house, all the while imagining what it could be that Mr. Bennett would say to her.

By the end of breakfast, her tension had mounted to the point at which she could wait no longer. She checked first to see if her father was in his study, then walked out in search of him. After checking the stables and outbuildings, she turned back toward the house in time to see him drive up in the curricle with his bailiff.

"Papa," she called, as she hurried toward his carriage, "had you any thought of going to the rectory today?"

"And good morning to you, Claire," he teased her gently as he climbed stiffly down. Claire smiled at him and gave him a kiss upon the cheek. "Nothing would please me more than to be able to go," he said, "but it seems that we have a problem with the estate. No, nothing for you to concern yourself with," he assured her, as she looked worried, "but it is something I should handle myself."

Claire managed to hide her disappointment, smiling casually at him and Mr. Spradling, the bailiff. "What about later?" she asked. "Is there any chance you would be free after you conclude your business?"

He considered. "I'm afraid this will take some time, but I can't be certain. Perhaps I will be finished by late morning. Is there any particular reason that you need to go today?"

"Not really," Claire admitted. "But since Lord Sitchville's ball is tomorrow, I won't be able to go then." This was true and made her all the more eager to go now.

"Oh, yes, I had forgotten that," said Lord Oliver. "Well, the best I can promise you is that I will try to hurry with my business and perhaps we will be able to go later."

"Thank you, Papa," said Claire, smiling in an attempt to appear unconcerned. She started back towards the house, frustrated at the delay. She worried that they might not get the chance to go this day, and that, even if they did, the visit might be so hurried as to prevent her from talking to Mr. Bennett privately. She turned abruptly.

"Papa," she called, "would you have any objection to my riding over there and waiting for you to join us? I am feeling rather out of sorts, and the ride will do me some good."

Lord Oliver looked at her searchingly for a moment, and Claire tried her best to look as though his answer would not seriously matter to her.

"Surely there could be no objection," she repeated.

Her father returned to his normal briskness. "Of course not," he agreed. "I will come to fetch you as soon as I have finished with Spradling here. Do not take all of the best books," he teased. "Have some thought for your old father."

She smiled lovingly at him and started off for the house to change into her riding habit.

Claire redressed her hair, brushing it out first, then pulling it up and fastening it on the top of her head with tortoiseshell combs. The ends fell down in ringlets on all sides.

She put on a forest-green wool riding dress, with bunched sleeves, the only puffs at the shoulders. The bodice was military in style and ended in a V with braid descending in loops on both sides from the shoulders to the waist. Her collar was turned up with a ruffled betsie beneath it; the skirt had loops of braid around the hem.

She put on the matching green hat, which resembled a top hat except for the plumes in back and the scarf around the brim. Then, taking her riding crop and her short kid gloves, she headed downstairs, stopping by the morning room to tell her mother that she would be riding over to the rectory, with Papa "just behind." Lady Sally was absorbed in letter writing and waved her off with a distant smile.

The ride to the rectory was refreshing after such a poor night's sleep, and Claire could feel the colour returning to her cheeks. The morning sun was almost too strong for her wool dress, but the breeze refreshed her as she rode.

Arriving at the rectory, she made straight for the stable to leave her horse, feeling rather odd to be seen coming on her own, but she smiled at Mr. Bennett's groom, whom she knew by now, as though her lone arrival were an everyday occurrence.

"Could you stable my horse for me please, Gurney? I shall be meeting my father here shortly, so you may expect him." The groom touched his cap to her, for he had grown to respect both her riding ability and her ladylike manner, and if he thought anything odd about her arrival, he did not let on.

Claire's heart beat a trifle faster as she proceeded to the house, fearing that the rector's butler might truly frown on her actions. But that most correct gentleman received her with his usual degree of respect and announced her to Mr. Bennett.

He was in his study and did not appear to be occupied with anything in particular, just staring off into space, which was unlike him, Claire thought. When he heard her name, he leaped eagerly to his feet, and Claire felt her heart jump in a response so strong that she could no longer fool herself as to its meaning. She felt flushed with the excitement of seeing him and lowered her head as he came to meet her, hoping not to give herself away.

I love him, she thought with a confused kind of happiness, *and he cares for me. How could I not have realized it before?* The impropriety of her being there alone suddenly struck her, for the difference in their stations and her own forwardness were now of great importance. She began to speak rapidly to hide her nervousness.

"It must seem very odd to you, my arriving like this, but the day was so fine that I decided to go for a ride. And my father expressed a wish to come see you, so I thought that I would join him here," she fabricated. "Has he not arrived yet?"

Mr. Bennett had walked forward to meet her, recovering control of his own expression after the surprise of seeing her, for he had been thinking of none other. He found it almost impossible not to respond to the joy in her face, but it confirmed what he had seen for the first time the day before—that Claire was falling in love with him as he had with her.

The time had come for him to make her understand how he must carry on and why, but the pleasure of having her here now to himself was so great he could barely speak. He had to turn away once she was greeted and walk to the window to gain control of his senses.

"You are always welcome; you know that," he said with no warmth in his voice. "Did you say your father would be along in a minute?"

"Why, yes, of course," said Claire with a bashful smile. She was feeling more embarrassed by the minute, knowing that her father might say something to expose her folly. The fact that Mr. Bennett had turned his back to her was alarming also, and the coldness in his voice was both surprising and upsetting.

"Perhaps it is as well," the rector said enigmatically. He turned to her, paused, and then went on, "We were interrupted yesterday before I had a chance to finish telling you something."

"I felt that," Claire began eagerly. This was more like what she had hoped for, but he raised a hand to stop her and smiled in an offhand way.

"Do not refine too much upon it. You will see that it is of little interest, but we have been such good friends that I felt a need—for myself, you understand—to let you know more about my circumstances."

The indifference in his voice chilled Claire. Her manner became grave and she again waited without comment to hear the rest of his story.

"I explained to you," he began, "the events that led to my taking a position in the Church, and I think you know from the things you have learned of me how I mean to go about it. I have not made many friends by doing things the way I do—you and your family are the glorious exceptions—but I do not mean to let that sway me."

He laughed, but it sounded bitter to Claire. She watched him as he began to pace the length of the room, keeping a good distance from her.

"I have been disillusioned by many things in my life. My cousin was more or less a stranger to me because of the difference in our ages, and I saw little of him until my father died and I became his ward. I knew that he did not get on well with my uncle. But I have to admit that his character was a surprise, even a shock, to one who was supposed to call him cousin.

"He conceived an instant dislike for me, whether it was jealousy of his father's fondness for me I do not know, and it does not really matter. Suffice it to say that for whatever reason, he took a certain pleasure in tormenting me.

"I have already told you of some of the ways he managed to stifle my ambitions. What I didn't say was how much pleasure he showed at my frustration. I am almost certain that he purchased my commission in a regiment going to America with the hope of seeing me killed; if not that, then at least for the purpose of preventing my acquiring any glory through military distinction. He is a clever man; his ignorance is entirely wilful."

Claire was turning pale with the pain she felt for the rector, and she at last understood the source of the sorrow she had always detected in him. She could not help herself from saying, "You sound as if you hate him."

"Do I?" he asked softly with irony in his voice. "Well, I do."

He waited a moment, then continued: "I know for a fact that he wanted a Church career for me for the pleasure he anticipated in seeing me toady to my benefactor. He used to joke often enough about it," he recalled bitterly. "It amused him to think of me sitting at the elbow of one of his friends, fawning for favours and running about eagerly to please his wife. But he made one mistake, my cousin. He used his influence to get a preferment for me, without stopping to think that it could not be taken away, no matter how I chose to use it."

The rector again paused, almost as if he could not make himself go on. At last he said quietly, "He joked that, if I did not like my situation, I might hang out for a rich wife."

There was nothing that Claire could say. His words dropped into the air like small pebbles into still water, but their ripples swept over her like a tidal wave. A small "Oh" escaped her lips, but Mr. Bennett refused to look at her.

He cleared his voice before speaking again.

"You are a reader of Miss Austen, are you not, Miss Oliver? I do not fancy myself a Mr. Wickham, nor even a Mr. Elton, and yet either of those two characters would have a happier wife than I am likely to have with the enemies I expect to make. Because of my calling, I cannot be denied the front door, but who would there be to stop someone from showing my wife or children to the back by way of insulting me?" He shook his head sadly. "I do not think I shall ever marry."

He seemed to feel that he had dwelt long enough on his own prospects for he turned to face her now, his expression under control, his look impersonal. "My cousin's poor wife died in childbirth. It must have been a blessed release for her, pitiable creature, for John treated her abominably. Now he has another, even younger. I pity her."

He fell silent then, and Claire felt herself incapable of speaking, but at length the rector broke the silence.

"You must think it strange of me to bring all this up," he said with an uncertain laugh, "but we have been such friends—that is, you and your parents have been so kind to me—that I wanted you to understand why I sometimes behave the way I do, or why I make certain decisions."

Claire smiled at him bravely. He had been completely honest with her, and though he had made no attempt to bind her to him, she knew in her heart that his pretence of indifference had cost him much effort. She felt that she owed him the same. It could serve neither of them to be more open with their feelings. His decision was made, and the integrity and independence that had caused him to make such a decision were two of the things she most loved about him. She would not have it otherwise.

"I cannot think what must be keeping my father," she said finally. "It is not like him to keep me waiting. I hate to go without him, but I have preparations to make for the ball tomorrow and should not tarry. You will tell him for me that I could not wait?" she asked.

Mr. Bennett nodded. It seemed that he had at last run out of words. For a moment, Claire felt that her shoes were weighted to the floor and she could not move. It was as though leaving that room would place a seal on all that had been said. Finally, though, she crossed the room to leave. He made no move to stop her, nor did he walk her to the door. She left the rectory as in a trance, somehow located her horse, mounted and rode off.

Christopher Bennett remained motionless as long as he could still hear the slightest sound that indicated her presence. It wasn't until the last hoofbeat was heard that he walked over to a chair and fell into it, his head in his hands.

She will marry that fool Babcock, he thought, and I will be here to see them, and watch them, until I can stand it no longer. Well, John, you really have won now, and in a way that you will never know. Then, his fists clenched, he declared, "And I will never let you know!"

He heard a sound in the hallway and raised his head just as Lord Oliver was announced. There was nothing he could do but explain to her father that Claire had already gone.

CHAPTER THIRTEEN

LORD OLIVER RETURNED to his home rather annoyed with his daughter. He had made an effort to conclude his business with all speed to accommodate her wish to go to the rectory, and she had not bothered to wait for him. It was possible, of course, that she had given up on him, but he had not taken all that long. Perhaps it was because Mr. Bennett had received her coldly. He certainly did not seem to be happy to see Lord Oliver, so the baron had left as soon as he could without seeming to be affronted. No doubt the young man had business to attend to.

Claire was nowhere downstairs when he got back to the house, so he waited till dinnertime to speak to her. But when she joined her parents at the table, she looked so unwell that he did not have the heart to reprimand her. She apologized, saying that she had continued to feel unwell in spite of her ride and had cut her visit short.

Her parents were worried about her, but they knew she did not want to be fussed over, so they expressed their loving sympathy and suggested she have a tray sent up to her room. Claire, who was finding it difficult to hide the reason for her misery from them, agreed and left the table.

Alone in her room, Claire lay on her bed and thought over Mr. Bennett's words. His revelations about his cousin had horrified her. It was impossible to think of there being anyone related to such a good man who could be so unfeeling, so cruel. Her mind dwelt lovingly on all his qualities. She could close her eyes and see his face before her smiling with swift understanding at one of her father's quips, frowning with intensity when talking about the working conditions for children. It was such a sensitive face.

She pictured all the lines around his eyes and his mouth. They had formed in all the right places, laugh lines for his splendid sense of humour and worry lines that showed how he cared about others. It was so hard to believe that anyone could hate him, as his cousin obviously did.

Claire knew that his concern for the welfare of others was sincere; it was as much a part of him as the lines of his face or his smile. He had to be true to his nature, no matter what the cost to himself or those around him. That was what he had said to her.

If he had given her the chance, if he had spoken of marriage to her, she would have told him that it made no difference to her if she were considered the "rich wife," that she would gladly have brought her fortune to him, that they could have used it to do the things he wanted to do. But he had not, and while she admired him for making that decision alone, she knew that in his place she could not have done the same.

All of this hurt, but what hurt most of all was the assumption she knew Mr. Bennett had made—that she would marry Lord Babcock. It was one thing to decide that he could not have her himself, for reasons of his own, but it was another to make a decision for her. Did he really think that she would marry Babcock? It made her so angry she could scream. Perhaps he thought it was already decided, as everyone else thought. But if he did not know that she loved him, why had he told her any of this?

All the rest of that day and for much of the night, Claire thought about the things they had said, the many times they had talked and strolled about the garden, their pleasure in the same activities and enjoyment in the same stories. But now all that had changed. He had deliberately placed a distance between them, and she understood why. He did not trust himself to be around her anymore.

The knowledge gave her a sense of power, but she knew that she must never use it. She must learn to be content with seeing him far less frequently, and probably never privately—but he would see after a time that there was nothing between her and Babcock!

By morning she was sleeping soundly. The tears she had expected had never come, but the ache in her throat was worse, and only the fatigue of hours of lying awake, tormented by her thoughts, had let her sleep. Lady Sally did not waken her because the ball was to be that evening and she hoped that with some additional rest Claire would feel up to going, and by early afternoon Claire had come downstairs and declared herself well enough to go. The Olivers exchanged worried glances because it was obvious that something was wrong. They knew instinctively that Claire was not ill, but they said nothing because they did not wish to meddle in her affairs. They knew that she would tell them if she wanted them to know.

When she left the room, Lord Oliver looked at his wife significantly and said, "Claire went to the rectory on her own yesterday."

Lady Sally responded at first, "Oh?" And then after a moment, "Oh! Oh, dear!" She looked truly concerned. "Do you think that I should speak to her?"

"No," replied Lord Oliver confidently. "Claire will know what is best to do." Still, he felt guilty for not having seen the signs before.

"Of course, you are right," said Lady Sally unhappily. She looked at him and he could see how she was suffering along with their daughter. "But he is such a nice man, and so handsome!"

Claire, meanwhile, hardly noticed the passage of the day, so lost in thought was she. Mostly her mind was occupied with a vision of a future without Christopher Bennett. She had thought her life a happy one before he came, but now she knew that something had been missing.

If only he had never come, she thought, I might have gone on contentedly forever.

But the future now stretched bleakly before her. She would return to the life she now saw as lonely. It was amazing that one could be surrounded by loving people and yet be lonely, but if the one person who mattered more than all others was absent, no amount of affection could make up for it. She began to understand that the isolated existence her family had always led was all right for her parents, for they had each other's love, a love she had not understood until now. But for her, the days would be forever the same; she would be forever alone.

As evening approached, Claire reluctantly began to prepare for the ball. She had looked forward to the evening with such delight, in spite of the prospect of uncomfortable scenes with Babcock, and now she knew why—it was the prospect of seeing Mr. Bennett. But now all her delight was gone, and she would have pleaded illness and stayed home, but such behaviour was unlike her and would have caused comment. And besides, what difference would one evening make when she was faced with a lifetime of loneliness?

The thought that Christopher might be at the ball was enough to make her dress with even more than her usual care. She put on a fresh chemise and one thin petticoat of cotton, trimmed with tucks and broderie anglaise. Bowing to fashion, she wore a soft corset which both nipped in the waist and supported the bust. Her stockings were white silk and her slippers the softest kid.

Her gown was of white satin, with off-the-shoulder puffed sleeves and a trim of fine lace stretching from the top of one sleeve across the *décolleté* neckline to the other sleeve. It clung tightly the full length of the bodice and almost to the hips before it began to flare, and a large white sash was tied in back at the waist. The only colour came from a row of red rosettes which began just under the right breast, descended and crossed diagonally over the front of the gown to the point where the skirt became fuller, then swooped gracefully into a triple row round the hem.

Claire dressed her hair with dainty red roses, the colour standing out dramatically against her black curls. She chose a locket of mosaic in favour of gold and pulled on a pair of long white kid gloves. Finally she put on her navy blue silk taffeta mantle with the wide collar, fastened with only a ribbon tie at the waist. It had a wool interlining, was lined with navy blue silk, and the edges were bound in navy blue velvet.

Surveying herself in the mirror, she could find fault only with her colouring, which was unusually wan, so she pinched her cheeks until tears sprang to her eyes, and it took all her power to put them to a stop—for they were caused by something far more painful than pinches to the skin....

Not far away in the Willoughby household, Lydia had got only to that stage of dress which found her face down on the floor, her mother's foot placed firmly on her back to get the proper purchase on the laces of her corset. It was a precaution that Sophia would never have foregone, and Lydia was unaware that not every young lady had to suffer the same. When at last she was thoroughly laced, tucked and padded, her mother dressed her hair high on her head, leaving long curls at the temples and shorter ones at the forehead.

Lydia dressed with much more excitement than Claire. Not only were such entertainments as the upcoming ball rarer in her restricted life, but she had reason to feel that something wonderful was about to happen. Lord Babcock had taken on the persona of a demigod for her. He had been so kind to her, so protective and respectful, all of the things an ideal man should be. She knew that he was intended for Claire, but the prospect of having just one dance with him was so exciting that she could hardly wait for the ball to begin. And he had hinted quite broadly that he would ask her to dance.

Sophia carefully lifted the ball gown over Lydia's head, the gown for which she had saved all her extra housekeeping money for a year. She saw the delight in her daughter's face and answered it with a loving smile, but she was anxious nonetheless. She could not bear to have her daughter hurt, and, regarding marriage as a worldly matter rather than a decision of the heart, she saw little hope for Lydia. Normally she would not have been able to refrain from a lecture on prudence and modesty, but she could not bear to erase the happy anticipation in Lydia's expression and so said nothing.

Sophia draped her own gold bracelets on her daughter's wrists and clasped a locket around her neck. Then she stepped back to observe the overall effect. Lydia's gown was of gold-coloured satin with bronze lace at the bosom and small bronze puffs for sleeves. The gold tones complemented Lydia's colouring perfectly, and a two-inch belt attracted the eye to her nipped-in waist. Over the dress, she was to wear a Spanish brown silk taffeta mantle, edged in black velvet pile and lined with matching brown glazed cotton.

Sophia, normally not at a loss for words, was speechless with pride. She wrapped Lydia's mantle gently around her, tied it, and held her daughter's cheek briefly against her own. They then smiled at one another and went to await the Olivers' carriage, which was to take them to the ball.

When their party arrived at Sitchville Park, it was to find the great hall transformed into a lavish ballroom. An orchestra was set up on the dais where the head table had been before, chairs were placed around the room's perimeter, and the rest was left for the dancers. The Olivers and the Willoughbys were greeted by Lady Sitchville, who once again had taken a position near the door to the vestibule.

Theresa Sitchville was entertaining some of her guests with the latest bit of news from London, and Lady Sally stopped with Claire to listen. Claire vaguely remembered hearing a shot from the mail coach that afternoon, but she had been too preoccupied to take notice of it. Apparently the news had been exciting.

"It was about the Duchess of Kent's new baby—I told you, I believe, that it was a girl," she repeated for the Oliver ladies. "Well, it seems that the Regent attended her christening, much to Kent's dismay. And of course, then he had to be asked for a name. Kent, you know—quite insensitively I think—suggested the name Charlotte, which angered the prince dreadfully. Then, apparently he took so long to think of a name for her that everyone became quite embarrassed—the archbishop was left holding the child for the longest time!—and the duchess was ready to dissolve in tears. So the Regent finally said, 'Let her be called for her mother,' just like that, and so they named the baby Victoria. Isn't that amusing?"

"A most amusing story, Theresa," said Lady Sally, "and so like the Regent." They passed on into the hall before she commented to Claire, "Isn't it just like Prinny to ruin a child's christening! He must have been struggling to find a name that was not exactly regal, just to punish Kent. Well, it's still a lovely name and I don't suppose it much matters."

Claire had been looking around the room, hoping to see the rector, but he was not in evidence. She noticed Babcock in a distant corner speaking to some of his guests and was relieved at least to have some peace before she should be obliged to converse with him. It was not until the music began that Lord Babcock crossed to Claire and claimed her for the opening dance, as was his custom.

At all the previous balls and assemblies that they had both attended, Babcock had taken care to reserve specific dances with Claire in advance—always the first dance of the evening and the first waltz. This had become so expected by the people present that other young men had stopped asking Claire for those dances. This time, however, he had not spoken to her in advance and, taken up with her own thoughts, Claire had not thought about it until the moment he took her hand to lead her to the floor.

How like him, she thought annoyed, to assume that the dance would not be spoken for. But she was too troubled, too down at heart, to dwell on Babcock's lack of courtesy.

Her dance with Babcock was soon over, and Claire was relieved that he did not remain at her side, but left to play host to other guests. She was quickly engaged for the second and third dances and tried to be cheerful for the sake of her partners, gentlemen she had known for some time. It was during the third dance that Christopher Bennett entered the room.

His eyes found her as quickly and as surely as a magnet finds metal. They looked at each other directly for only a moment before the dance led her away, but Claire was certain that he had been thinking about her when he entered. By the time she came round again, he was making his way towards some acquaintances.

She noticed once again how he appeared to advantage in knee breeches, with his finely muscled calves. His tailcoat and waistcoat were single-breasted and dark, his breeches, silk stockings, shirt and cravat a contrasting white. Claire, peeping surreptitiously at him from time to time, couldn't help but admire his powerful yet graceful carriage.

Christopher Bennett, too, had considered not coming to the ball, despite the disfavour his absence would incur from the Sitchvilles. He really had no other purpose in coming than to see Claire, but he wondered immediately if it had been wise. She was so lovely in her gown that the sight of her tore at his heart. It was a deliberate punishment he had dealt himself, he admitted, a delicious kind of torture to see her but not to have her. He engaged a young lady for the following dance, but planned to leave the ball as soon as decency permitted.

The fifth dance was the first waltz and Claire waited without caring or thinking for Lord Babcock to approach her. They were normally the first couple on the floor for a waltz, because Babcock had always made his approach to her such a ceremony that others had stepped aside to watch. Automatically the crowd waited for him to begin.

Babcock, however, had been waiting for this moment. Without caring what it might mean to Claire, he had planned what he thought of as a crucial move to show publicly that his affections had transferred. With his heart on his sleeve and in anticipation of a magical moment, he walked more humbly than was his wont over to Lydia and bowed. She blushed with happiness and surprise, and curtsied before accepting his hand. Then he led her proudly onto the floor.

It would be an exaggeration to say that a gasp went round the room, but it was noticed almost immediately that Claire had been left standing at the side of the hall. The ladies began to whisper in shocked tones and it was only a matter of moments before Mr. Bennett understood what had happened. He gritted his teeth angrily. He did not know why Claire had committed herself to Babcock, but he was not going to let that insufferable fool humiliate her in public.

Claire, who had barely registered that Babcock had left her in an awkward position, was just beginning to realize that people were staring at her and whispering. Her sorrow was such that Lord Babcock's display mattered little to her, although she was beginning to wish that the others would not stare so. Just then, Mr. Bennett appeared at her side.

"I believe that you promised me this dance, Miss Oliver," he said as he smiled and bowed.

Claire was thrilled at the protectiveness of his action. She blushed with lowered eyes, but then forced herself to look at him, and all of her feelings for him were visible in her answering smile. The beauty of her lovely expression caused a wrenching tug at his heart, but he kept his face impassive as he took her hand. Claire in her turn managed to fight back the sudden tears that sprang to her eyes.

They waltzed as neither of them had ever waltzed before. Claire was accustomed to the impersonal feel of a man's stiff hand on her back, but the rector's hand was not stiff. It was warm and strong, like an embrace around her waist. She had never been this physically close to him, and she felt for the first time the desire to melt into a man's arms. She felt a warm pulse start inside her; her heart beat rapidly and disturbingly. She had to focus on the pearl pin in his cravat to avoid losing her attention to the steps of the dance.

For his part, Christopher Bennett was sadly savouring every moment of the dance. Though she would not look up at him, he kept his eyes on the top of her hair to take with him the memory of her black locks entwined with red roses. When he allowed his gaze to drop to her gleaming white shoulders, he wanted nothing more than to cover them with kisses. The longing was almost more than he could bear and it made him clasp her waist more tightly. She felt him pull her toward him and she gasped and looked up.

For a split second, their eyes met, and they exchanged unguarded looks. For both of them it was a gripping moment; their passion for each other was revealed. Claire hastily looked away at the same instant the dance ended. Her eyes fixed on Christopher's extended arm, she took it and walked back with him to the edge of the floor. Hesitating a second, he bowed and walked away. Only then did she dare to look up again.

Her gaze followed him to the other end of the hall. His figure dominated the room. She could still imagine his arm around her and feel its strength, and she tried to stay in this dream state so that the memory would not fade. But her next partner came up and broke into her reverie, forcing her to give half her mind to the present.

Claire longed to go home so that she would have time to herself to think about Christopher, what he had just done to save her embarrassment, the look he had given her. Her heart leaped as she remembered it, and it was a memory she wanted to cherish throughout the coming months and years. But she could not leave yet and the evening stretched long before her.

Christopher felt no such social obligation. He had done the one thing he had come to do and now saw no reason to stay. The waltz with Claire had had an unsettling effect on him, which he was at pains to conceal. He had held her in his arms, and losing her now was going to be even harder to bear. The look they had exchanged had proven that her feelings were as intense as his own, and it had only made him want her more. But it could not change the circumstances.

As the rector approached the rear of the hall, he saw Robert Willoughby slip out the glass doors unnoticed by the other guests. It gave him the idea of taking a turn in the garden to collect himself before calling for his carriage, and so he followed him openly. But when he got outside, planning to avoid Robert, he saw that the other man was rapidly walking toward the stables, looking guiltily over his shoulder.

Normally Christopher would not have thought it his business to follow him, but he had not liked Tucker the one time he had seen him and he was concerned about the influence the trainer obviously had on Robert. He also felt the need for something to take his mind off his problems. He realized that Robert had not seen him exit the hall because of the shadows cast by the enormous turrets, so he waited for a few moments until Robert was out of sight, then walked slowly down to the stables.

By the time he arrived and entered the building, it seemed Robert was concluding his discussion with Tucker and was almost ready to return to the ball. But the conversation the rector overheard immediately upon entering was such that he decided to conceal his presence and try to learn more. Robert Willoughby was handing a small bundle over to Tucker.

"All right, there it is, man," he was saying testily. "I told you I would get it to you by tonight, didn't I."

Mr. Bennett could see the gleam in Tucker's eye from where he was concealed. "Coo, guv'nor, don't get in a quirk. How was I to knows you wouldn' come crab over me? I'm not used to dealing with no swell cove like yourself."

"If you mean by that that you couldn't trust me— and I'll never understand why you lackeys don't just speak English—how am I supposed to know that you won't squeak on me? Can you tell me that?" asked Robert.

"Now don't go suspicioning me, guv'nor," said Tucker in an offended voice. "It won't be me as 'll whiddle the scrap."

"Well—" Robert sounded mollified "—you shouldn't. It's not every day I turn over four hundred pounds to a man in your position. You're sure about everything, now, are you?" he asked uncertainly.

"Now, don't I knows that you'll comb my hair with a joint stool if anything goes wrong? It won't be me what catches cold, you can wager a coachwheel on it. I've got something special planned for this bang-up prancer—never you mind what," he said, jerking his head at Sarravano.

"It won't really hurt him, will it?" asked Robert anxiously, while petting Lord Sitchville's prospective Derby winner on the muzzle.

"Never you think such, guv'nor! You ought'er know better than that! Think I'd do anything that might put him to bed with a shovel?" Tucker sounded offended. "A cull like me what makes his livin' off o' horses? He'll be in prime twig in a brace o' snaps."

"All right, then." Robert sounded reassured. "You'll put the money on Magnifico to win, as we planned."

"Just leave everything to me and keep your mummer close," said Tucker. "I know what I'm doin'."

I'll bet he does, thought Mr. Bennett. At last he understood what Robert's ineffectual soul-searching had been all about. He and Tucker planned to drug Sarravano to ensure that the colt—clearly the favourite—would lose, and lose badly. Then he would bet a large sum of money on Magnifico, Sarravano's only real rival, and with the odds favouring Sarravano to win, Robert would stand to make a good deal of money. Lord Sitchville, and everyone going with the safe bet, would be the losers.

"In a few more days, you'll be a richer cove," Tucker was saying now.

The thought restored Robert to his cheerful self. "Well, it won't be a fortune," he said, partially to himself, "but it'll be a start. Won't I laugh to see Sitch lose his shirt for once," he added gleefully. Then, remembering that his absence from the ballroom would be noticed by his wife, he began to leave, reminding

Tucker that he would be back in a few days to collect his winnings, and adjuring him not to make any mistakes.

"They'll never twig my lay. I'm up to slum," Tucker replied as Robert disappeared out the door, unaware that he passed within a few feet of the rector.

Mr. Bennett continued to watch Tucker for a few minutes before speaking. Not to his surprise, Tucker began to laugh softly to himself the second Robert was out of earshot.

"Sure, you can count on me," the man said aloud to himself. "What fools, you flash coves are," he sneered. "A cool four hun'erd quid fer meself and nothin' fer you." Then he laughed again.

"I think not," said Mr. Bennett coolly as he stepped out from his place of concealment.

Tucker whipped around, anger and fear mingled on his face. He grabbed an iron hook which was hanging near his hand and swung it wildly at the rector before looking to see just who had spoken. Christopher dodged the hook easily, grabbed it as it went by and twisted the thing from Tucker's hand to throw it across the stable and out of reach. The anger and frustration he had felt due to the situation with Claire, long suppressed, burst out now that it had been given a target. He grabbed Tucker's shirt by the neck, lifted him into the air and shoved him against the wall, then subdued the man entirely with a single blow from his clenched right hand.

Tucker lay on the floor groaning and clutching his head with both hands. Christopher watched him for a few moments until he felt his own equanimity return;

then he pulled the trainer to his feet by the front of his shirt.

"Don't mill me down again, guv'nor!" pleaded Tucker, cowering.

"You are safe enough now, if you don't try any of your tricks again," said the rector.

"There now, your worship, I didn't know it was you," Tucker begged.

Christopher's calm had completely returned and he relaxed his grip on Tucker's shirt. "A simple 'sir' will suffice. I am not a bishop, you know. Though I don't suppose it would have stopped you from trying to gouge out my eyes if I had been," he said dryly.

"How was I to know you wasn't no hedge-bird with a barking iron come to prig milord's horse here?" said Tucker in his most reasoning tone. "I was mistook, that's all. No need to put yourself in a quirk."

"You can dispense with the story, Tucker," Christopher said wearily. "I heard the whole plot and you will never be able to convince me that you are not a most unsavoury character. I expect you know that. Now. Hand over the money."

Tucker realized in a second that the rector knew of his plot. He turned pale. "Give me yer hand, yer honner—I'm gonna shoot the cat," he said pitifully.

Seeing the pallor in the groom's face, and realizing he was indeed about to lose his dinner, Christopher helped him over to a bale of hay and told him to lie down—still watching him carefully, however. He waited until Tucker's colour returned before speaking again.

"You needn't try to gammon me again. I'm not the halfling you think. I'll have the money now," the rector said, extending his hand.

"I wasn't going to hurt the horse, sir, I swear I wasn't," Tucker said rapidly, hoping somehow to keep the money. The rector looked implacably at him. There was no impatience in his demeanour, but Tucker knew that he had lost.

"It near breaks my heart to part with such a roll o' soft," he said sadly, handing over Robert's money.

"You should have thought about that before you took it," was the rector's only comment.

"How was I to know you was such a fly cove?" asked Tucker defensively. "It's not like you was likely to twig my rig, not a nib cove like you. How did you know?" he asked.

"It only took one meeting with you to see that something havey-cavey was afoot," said Mr. Bennett wearily. "It was only a matter of time."

Tucker's look became ugly again. "An' what's it to you if I want to tap a shy one on the shoulder? That fat old gager deserves what he gets."

"Undoubtedly he does," Christopher replied, "but that doesn't mean you should be the one to benefit by it. And you may take it as an unwarranted kindness on my part that I do not report you to the magistrate."

"You're not going to call in the boman prigs?" asked Tucker incredulously. "Don't try to gammon me, guv'nor."

"You have my word on it," the rector assured him. "I have no particular fancy to see your face up on the gallows every time I go to market for the next month or so."

Tucker paled at the thought. "What'll I do now, guv'nor?"

Mr. Bennett looked at him thoughtfully. "You may stay on as you are," he said after a moment, "as long as you remember that I will be watching you and will know if you are up to something. I cannot guarantee that I will be so kindly disposed the next time, so it would be in your interest to behave."

Tucker was dumbfounded. He felt a need for explanation. "I wouldn'a taken to this lay if times hadn'a been so rough, guv'nor. It's not much better than a monkey's allowance they gives you here," he added bitterly.

"You have a roof over your head and food to eat," said Mr. Bennett curtly. "That is more than many people can say. I would not be so quick to despise it." He was weary of Tucker's bitter company. Placing Robert's wad of money in his coat pocket, he nodded curtly to the groom and left the stables.

CHAPTER FOURTEEN

LORD BABCOCK had enjoyed the ball immensely. After his first daring waltz with Lydia, he had not looked back. He had danced with her twice more, and had, in short, made something of a spectacle of his feelings for her. But that had not deterred him; the feel of her in his arms made him oblivious to the stares of the other guests.

He had not been oblivious to his mother's stares, but he had carefully avoided looking at her, and whenever she had approached him he had made sure that someone else was too close for her to speak freely. Most of the evening he had been able to avoid talking to her at all, and he had made sure that she was gone to bed before he had completely dropped his guard.

The afternoon following the ball found him dreamily sipping his chocolate and humming one of the waltzes. It was as he was lowering the cup from his lips that his mother appeared for her breakfast and barked at him in a voice he had never heard before.

"Cecil!" The severity of this greeting caused him to lose his mouthful of cocoa in a fine spray over his mother's linen tablecloth. His hand began to shake, causing the cup to clatter in its saucer. He hastily put it down and tried to appear innocent.

"Good morning, Mama." He smiled nervously. "I hope you enjoyed a good night's rest."

His mother did not appear mollified. "I hope you realize," she said, "that I will not be able to sleep or hold my head up in this county until you right your disgraceful behaviour of last night."

Her son looked shocked. Had it really been all that bad?

"How could you have behaved so?" his mother asked before he had a chance to deny anything. "You have slighted your intended bride unpardonably."

Babcock decided not to pretend he did not know to whom she was referring. "I protest, Mama. I led Miss Oliver out for the first dance, as was proper."

"Only to make a spectacle of yourself by then dancing three—I counted three!—dances with Miss Willoughby, and no more with Claire. It will not do, Cecil."

Lord Babcock decided to be straightforward. "Mama," he began stoutly, "I have decided that I will not be happy with Miss Oliver as my wife."

"Happy!" exclaimed his mother. "We are not put on this earth to be happy," she remarked scornfully.

"Of course not, Mama," agreed Babcock respectfully. His mother was always reasonable. There was no point in telling her that he was in love with Lydia. That was not at issue.

Lady Sitchville knew what was in his mind, but she could not relent. The Sitchville name was what mattered uppermost.

"You will call on Lord Oliver and Lady Sally this afternoon," she ordered. "You will make your request for Claire's hand. It has gone on long enough, and this will put an end to it.''

Lord Babcock's heart sank, but he knew better than to argue. He had his duty.

"As you wish, Mama.'' He sighed.

As his appetite was by now gone, he rose and went to his room to prepare for his call on Claire. He chose his most sombre day attire, a dull grey. He reflected that if he had been going to propose to Lydia, he would have worn his new, spotted, mauve waistcoat.

Claire had been sitting at a window near the front of the house since breakfast, trying to keep her attention on the book in her hands. It was hard to understand the words when her heart was following the rhythm of the waltz in her head. For in spite of the apparent hopelessness of her love for Christopher, she was still elated by the memory of that dance. It had tapped a joy within her that had never before been tapped, and her efforts to control it with logic were failing.

It was in this mood that she heard a caller at the door. For a moment she thought it might be the rector, but her spirits dropped like a stone when she saw Lord Babcock enter the room. Her parents were still upstairs, having been worn out by the previous evening, so she had to receive him alone. This did not disturb Babcock, though she could tell that his mind was in a turmoil. After her greeting, he began to pace the room in an agitated manner.

"Claire,'' he began at last, "I mean M-m-miss Oliver. No, dash it, Claire!'' he said firmly.

"My lord!'' Claire exclaimed in mock indignation. If she had thought by this to squelch any further intention of his to speak, it did not work. He did not acknowledge her response, and Claire could see that he was in a frenzy of composition. She decided to let him take his time.

"We have known each other for quite a long time," he said in a cajoling tone. "We have always been such pleasant friends...."

His words trailed off as if he did not really know where to go from there.

Claire turned away to hide the smile on her face. It appeared as though Babcock were here to propose, but she could tell right away that this was not how he would begin if that were his intention. She could help him out of his difficulty by stopping him, but a small demon in her could not resist prolonging his discomfort.

"Is that all we have been?" she asked in a pitiful voice, her back still to him. "Friends?"

Babcock was horrified. His mother was right! This was going to be every bit as difficult as he had feared. Was he really going to have to marry the girl?

"Of course, that is, the very best of friends, of course," he babbled. "You must know by now that I cherish the greatest respect for you, a great warmth of feeling that I can only consider—" Babcock had been going to say "fraternal," but Claire spoke before he had the chance.

"My lord, you honour me," she said, her voice sounding as if she were overcome by emotion and her hand held out behind her as if for him to take it.

Babcock gazed at that hand with horror. He had to clarify matters.

"No, I don't!" he squeaked. "I mean, of course, that I do—that is, you mustn't think of it that way," he pleaded.

Claire was enjoying herself enormously. She wanted to turn around to see the expression on his face, but she was afraid to give herself away.

"How can I not?" she asked, gratitude in her voice. "All your *manifold* attentions, your kindness. *So* obvious, too. Everyone must be aware of them."

"Surely not!" Babcock protested desperately. "You know how people will talk, er, exaggerate! My attentions to you have been in no way, er, exceptional, I think. Quite normal, in fact. Yes, quite normal." Babcock hoped that this described them accurately.

"Yes, I suppose under the circumstances, they have," said Claire, and before Babcock could ask what "circumstances," she turned dramatically towards him and smiled affectionately with her arms outstretched. The look of fear on his face caused her to turn her back again rapidly to hide her mirth.

"Circumstances?" was all he managed to say in a strangled voice.

"You need not attempt to conceal your feelings," she answered. "I have been aware of them for some time now." And to his alarm, she began to weep quietly.

"You have?" he asked, astonished. "How did you know? That is, you mustn't let it distress you. I did not mean to cause you pain; you must understand that. Perhaps I have acted foolishly, but I didn't know...you must believe me...this has been all so unexpected. My parents...but I," Babcock strove to say the correct thing, but he was so confused by now that he had no idea what that might be.

"My pain!" exclaimed Claire in mournful tones. "You speak of my pain!" Again she turned to face him, deciding that it was time for one more twist of the knife, and then mercy.

"You who have been so noble and have done me such an honour."

Babcock thought, have I proposed? I don't remember.... He was perspiring profusely.

"But it will not do," Claire continued. "I cannot bear to have you go on, knowing the pain that you will soon feel. I am so loath to wound you, but I must. You will forever have my gratitude, but I cannot do as you wish."

"My pain?" Babcock asked in a fog, unable to make head nor tail of the conversation.

"I cannot accept your kind offer," Claire said with finality.

"You can't?" said Babcock, unsure whether to be pleased or affronted.

"No," said Claire. "There is ... another." She said this dramatically just for the effect, but it made her think of Christopher, and her heart leapt perversely as her mind sobered.

"Well!" exclaimed Babcock, not knowing quite how to take this information. But as his mind cleared from the confusion of the past many minutes, he began to feel relief. He was able at last to respond with grace.

"This comes as a grave blow to me, as you must know," he said, but second by second, he was beginning to feel the joy that release and new hope can bring. Trying to keep a sombre face, he backed towards the door, unable to wait any longer to leave. "I will always preserve the greatest affection for you in my heart." This was delivered in great haste as he backed out the door. Hardly staying for his "Good day" to be returned, he ran out the door of the house, calling for his horse.

Claire waited, holding her breath, for the sound of his horse galloping away. Then she burst out in laughter. The burden of years had been lifted and she had enjoyed every second of the episode. She could not stand to keep the joke to herself any longer, however, and ran upstairs to share it with her parents.

Lord Babcock, meanwhile, was heading toward Sitchville Park in a state of happy bewilderment, but suddenly he reined in his horse. He hesitated for only a moment before changing his direction to coincide with the route to the Willoughby cottage. "We are not put on this earth to be happy," his mother had said. But surely there was no harm in it if it just so happened! His hesitation had been over whether to return to the house for his mauve waistcoat, but in spite of feeling at a disadvantage without it, he decided he would somehow manage.

Less than half an hour later, the Honourable Robert Willoughby walked into his drawing room to be greeted by the almost hysterical raptures of his wife and the sight of his daughter holding hands with Lord Babcock in front of the fireplace. It was quickly explained to him that his daughter was to have the honour of marrying the young man who stood before him, happiness and pride in his demeanour.

Robert could not speak. His good fortune struck him dumb and he fell into the closest chair before he could take it all in. Sophia chastised him for not expressing his consent for the match, so he hastened to give it.

"Of course, of course," he assured them. "It's just caught me by surprise. I never knew there was anything going in that direction," he continued ingenuously, unaware of the embarrassment Babcock was likely to feel.

"I was too afraid to aspire so high," Lord Babcock said with evident sincerity, bowing to kiss Lydia's hand. She blushed with happiness.

"Yes, yes," Robert said dismissively, uncomfortable with flowery expressions of young love. "All very right and proper, I'm sure. Well, we will be happy to count you among the family, young man," he said, rising to his feet and clapping Babcock on the back. He could already envision the possibilities of such a connection. He planned to become quite close with Lord Sitchville, his future fellow father-in-law.

Sophia was obviously in seventh heaven. Her Lydia, her pride and joy, was making a match that would throw all others in the shade. And to such a young man! His fortune was staggering, but on top of that he was a model of propriety. She could not have been happier.

Robert was feeling the glow of better prospects; he was even, for once, in complete accord with his wife. They smiled at each other with their first shared joy in many years.

There was much congratulation all round, and mooning looks exchanged by the young people. Sophia was too strict to let them be alone, so eventually Lord Babcock was forced to take his leave without a private moment with his love. He bid them a reluctant farewell.

"You cannot imagine my regret at having to leave home at such a time, but it will only be for a few days."

"You're off somewhere?" asked Robert in a voice of paternal bonhomie.

"Why, yes," answered Babcock, "to Epsom, for the Derby. Our horse is favoured to win, you know. In my opinion, he can't be beat." Then turning to his new fiancée, he bade a fond farewell, not noticing the suddenly greenish hue of his future father-in-law's face.

CHAPTER FIFTEEN

IT WAS WELL INTO THE AFTERNOON when Claire, having resumed her reading, was interrupted by Robert Willoughby. He dashed into the room, desperation in his face.

"Uncle Bobby!" Claire exclaimed. "Whatever is the matter?"

Robert looked about him distractedly, hardly knowing where to begin. He whispered anxiously, "Where are your parents?"

Claire relaxed a bit. It was obvious to her that no one had been hurt, as had been her first fear. Robert was frightened of being caught out in something, a much less disturbing occurrence.

"You need not worry," she told him. "They have gone upstairs and are both resting."

Robert sat down suddenly by her and grabbed her hand. "You've got to help me, Claire. The most terrible thing has happened."

His obvious anxiety alarmed her again. He had never spoken to her this way before, no matter what his scrapes.

"What is it, Uncle Bobby? Of course, I will help you. What has happened?"

Robert looked her squarely in the eyes, his face white with fear. He rasped, "Babcock has offered for Lydia."

Claire waited for one second, then burst out laughing. She was surprised to see that her uncle's expression was still the same.

"I will admit, Uncle Bobby, that the news might be enough to cause some alarm," she said when she could again speak, "but is that any cause for this degree of anxiety?"

Robert shook his head impatiently. "No! No!" Then he said with greater control, "That's not the trouble. I'm no fool. The match couldn't be better. Lydia fancies him, too, it's plain to see. It's just caught me all off guard. I wasn't expecting it." He wrung his hands, clearly disturbed.

"Then I am afraid that I do not see the problem." Claire was searching for some reason for his behaviour. "Surely Aunt Sophia cannot object!" she exclaimed.

"Of course not, girl! Use your head! She thinks he hung the moon. No. The problem is the Derby!" Desperation was again in his voice. "You've got to help me. Something must be done or I'll be ruined. I'll never be able to explain to Sophia. She'll kill me, or if she doesn't someone else will. You've got to help me!"

Claire's heart sank to hear him mention the Derby. Horses were his greatest weakness. She knew his capacity for getting into trouble, though she still did not see how it related to Babcock's proposal to Lydia.

"You've got to tell me what you have done, Bobby," she said firmly, "if I am going to be any help to you. It has something to do with the Derby, does it?''

"That's what I've been telling you, isn't it?" he asked impatiently. "It's the money. I've got to get the money back from Tucker. Call the whole thing off."

"Tucker!" exclaimed Claire. So this was what her uncle had been doing in Lord Sitchville's stable all this time. "What money have you given to Tucker?"

"For a bet," her uncle said, avoiding her direct look. "I told him to place a bet for me on a sure winner—and it's not Sitchville's colt. It's Sir George's."

Claire was puzzled. "But why would you do that? Lord Sitchville's horse is favoured to win, isn't he? And what difference would it make to Lord Babcock? It is not as though he would be likely to find out."

For once, her uncle looked ashamed. "Sitchville's horse is not going to win. Tucker is seeing to that."

It took a moment for the implication of these words to sink in. Then horror invaded Claire's mind.

"Uncle Bobby!" she gasped. "You didn't plan with Tucker to hurt Lord Sitchville's horse? Please tell me you didn't. How could you do such a thing?"

"I've told you," he said defensively. "I had no idea Babcock would be offering for Lydia! I thought he was angling after you." He worried suddenly that he might offend her, but Claire did not seem to have noticed.

"That's totally beside the point!" she exclaimed, astonished at his answer. "How could you be involved in something so dishonest?"

"I don't have time to worry about that now," said Robert anxiously. "You've got to help me stop Tucker before it's too late. I thought it would be funny to see Sitch lose a little on the races, but that was before I knew he would be my Lydia's father-in-law. Now it would be like taking the bread out of my own mouth."

"It would serve you right if you did," Claire admonished. "I don't see how anything can be done to stop it at this late date. It won't be pleasant for Lord Sitchville to lose the race, not to mention the money he bets on it. But he needn't know that you were involved in the scheme, I suppose, for Lydia's sake."

Robert snorted, "Not know! He'll know all right if he gets wind of how much *I* win on the race. He's bound to put two and two together. I should have realized it before, but that fool Tucker made it sound so easy," he complained.

Claire experienced a further sinking in her stomach. "Uncle Bobby," she asked soberly, "how much money did you wager?"

He answered reluctantly, "Four hundred pounds."

Claire sprang to her feet. "I must call Papa. He can help try to stop Tucker!"

"You can't do that, girl!" exclaimed Robert. "Where do you think I got the money? Your father'll cut me off!"

Claire looked at him furiously. "You borrowed four hundred pounds from my father to use on a crooked scheme?"

"Of course not—at least, not all at once." Bobby had the grace to look sheepish. "A little here, a little there—you know how it is."

"No, fortunately I do not," she answered firmly. But she turned back from the door. He was right. She could not tell her father. It would cause a rift in the family, justifiably perhaps, but such a rift would only hurt her mother. Somehow, though, Tucker had to be stopped, or Lydia's match to Lord Babcock might be ruined. In truth they all stood to suffer if this came to light.

"You cannot ride after Tucker? Catch up to him?" she asked Robert. "You could borrow one of our horses."

"No," he answered. "I'm too old to go riding off as fast as I would have to go to catch them. If you can't think of something else, I'm a ruined man." He sank back hopelessly in his chair.

"Too old," mused Claire aloud. She would go herself if she were a man. What they needed now was a young strong man they could trust. Her heart leaped. Christopher Bennett. He was the person to help them. He had seen this coming, for he had worried that Bobby was getting mixed up in something shady. But she must explain it to him herself. Robert would take too long and with his twisted logic might not be able to persuade the rector to go.

"I have an idea," she told Bobby urgently as she hurried toward the door. "It's possible that someone can stop Tucker in time. I don't have time to explain," she said as she reached the door. "Just tell my parents that I have gone for a ride. I should be able to report something to you when I return." And to Robert's astonishment, she ran upstairs.

Claire dressed hastily for her ride to the rectory. She tried not to think about Christopher's possible reception of her, telling herself that she was doing it for Bobby, Lydia and Sophia. She could not let the feelings which she knew existed between them prevent her from seeking his help when she knew that he was the one person who truly could help.

Hurrying out to the stables, she gave her order to the groom, trying to appear as though nothing were out of the ordinary. Then she mounted and rode the short distance at a gallop. When she came in sight of the rectory, Claire rode directly to the stables, expecting to find his groom. It occurred to her that the man might think it strange for her to come again unattended. And this time, of course, she could not pretend that her father was close behind.

Well, she thought, her business would not take long, so there should not be too much conjecture about it.

But the rector's groom was not in the stable. After calling out to him a time or two she realized that he must be away on some errand, so after doing her best to stable her horse, she made for the house.

She saw, in the fading light of late afternoon, that the doors to Christopher's library were open to the garden and the light was on. Having felt self-conscious in her second appearance at the stables, she felt even more so at the prospect of meeting the butler with no excuse. In her haste, she had not prepared a story that did not sound lame to her own ears. She decided to walk up to the study doors to see if the rector was alone. Then it would be easy just to slip out the same way after speaking to him, and no one except him need ever know she had been there.

As Claire reached the door, she saw Christopher standing beside his desk. Her heart leaped and she realized how much she had longed to see him. As she hesitated in the doorway, however, wondering just how to make him aware of her presence, she saw something that drove all other thoughts from her mind.

He was looking at a letter he held in his hands, but what concerned her was the expression on his face. It was one of shock, as if the letter contained some news he could not believe. Claire felt the awkwardness of her position. She was certain that she would be noticed if she tried to slip away without entering, and at last, preferring not to be caught spying upon him, she stepped into the room.

Yet the news in the letter held the rector's attention so strongly that he did not at first notice her presence. Forgetting her own embarrassment, she stepped quite close to him, and said in a voice full of loving solicitude, "My dear, what is it?"

At that moment, and it was only then that he became aware of her presence, Christopher swung around, the look of shock still on his face. Without a word, he clasped her to him, holding her tightly as if for dear life.

For what seemed like minutes he held her thus without speaking, and Claire did not resist. It was heaven to her to be resting safe in his arms, even for just a moment. She had forgotten all about Bobby and Tucker, and her only thought was that something momentous must have happened to unsettle the rector, but whether it was good or bad she had no clue.

At last he drew back slowly, as though waking from a dream. She expected him to release her entirely, but instead he held her by the shoulders and looked searchingly into her eyes as he spoke.

"I love you," he said.

The simplicity of his statement and the tone of his voice took Claire's breath away. In them, she sensed the total breakdown of the barriers he had put between them, the effort they had cost him and the entreaty that it might not yet be too late to forget them.

Choked with emotion and unable to speak, she raised a hand to caress his cheek, and she smiled at him through her sudden tears.

Christopher's gaze locked with hers, and joy and relief swept through him. Without waiting to answer questions, he took her in his arms again and kissed her with all the pent-up feeling he had restrained for weeks and weeks. Claire responded with all her heart.

After a time, in which he kissed her again and again, but more gently, as if afraid to stop, he held her away from him and laughed unsteadily. In a low, husky voice, he said, "Does this mean you love me, Miss Oliver?"

"Oh, yes," she answered softly. "I always have."

Christopher pulled her back into his arms. It did not seem to be the time for explanations. He had wanted to hold her for so long.

After a while he forced himself to hold her away again. She had not drawn back, but he knew it was time to explain, and taking her by the hand, he led her to a small sofa. Claire unconsciously began rubbing the back of her neck, and he looked at her quizzically.

"Am I too tall for you?" he asked.

She blushed, finding it hard to meet his gaze, so suddenly had everything changed. "Perhaps a little," she admitted.

"We can remedy that," he asserted firmly and sitting down, he drew her onto his lap. Now their faces were at the same level, and Christopher could not resist kissing her once again.

Finally he sighed contentedly and released her. Claire knew he wanted to speak of his news but was finding it hard to know where to begin.

"You must have known that I loved you," he said. "It was probably from the first, though I was so absorbed with my purpose here that it was too late before I saw the danger to myself. I thought all along that I would not marry, could not in fact marry one such as you, but I did not realize at first that your heart might be in danger, too."

Claire assured him that it was by kissing him softly around his face. He smiled and went on.

"As soon as I realized what was happening, I tried to make you understand why it would be impossible for us to be happy together, even though I wanted you more than anything I've ever wanted in my life. Did you understand, Claire?" he asked, holding her tightly again as if to prove it.

"Yes," she said gently, "but something has happened to change all that, hasn't it." It was not a question, but a statement.

Christopher heaved a great sigh. It was pregnant with both the burden of having something to tell and with an enormous relief, which was nevertheless not free of pain.

At last he said, "My cousin is dead."

Claire did not know what to say. The news came as a total surprise to her, and the suddenness of it—the realization that all their pain of being apart could be ended by the death of someone—came as a shock to her.

Christopher looked apologetic. "I should have told you immediately," he said. "I should have said something before I took advantage of being with you. But I had just read the letter and, forgive me, the only thought in my mind at the moment was that now, perhaps, I would be free to love you. And then there you were. It was as though I had been granted a wish."

Claire, now that the shock was subsiding, hastened to reassure him. "Do not think that you behaved wrongly. You have never been a hypocrite and there is no reason to start being one now just because your cousin is dead. He gave you no reason to love him, and I shall not think better of him just because he is no longer here to torment you."

She paused a moment, then said, "And this came as a total surprise to you—" she hesitated again "—Christopher?" It pleased her to use his Christian name. She had used it in all her thoughts and now it was hers to speak. "You had no news that he was ill?"

"None at all," Christopher said, still incredulous. "He was never ill a day in his life that I know of. That was one of his most unattractive traits, somehow, that he was able to pursue his dissipation with such energy and never be the least bit weary." His tone was now quite matter-of-fact and Claire was happy to see him become more himself. She did not like to think of his feeling any guilt for not caring more about his cousin's death.

"He was thrown by a horse and broke his neck," he explained. "The letter said he died instantly. It was from his new wife," he added, "and I must say in my defence that she does not sound any more bereaved than I. And he did not suffer, she said, so we needn't be concerned with that."

The rector was completely himself once again. The shock of the news of his cousin's death had passed, and with no affection for the man to give him pain and no need to justify himself to Claire, he could now give his attention where he most wanted to give it. He hugged Claire tightly with a groan of satisfaction.

"Did you blame me for letting him stand between us?" he asked.

"No," replied Claire. "I knew that you would not be happy under those circumstances and I did not want anything that was wrong for you." She hesitated before speaking again. "I wanted to tell you that the matter of fortune would not weigh with me, and that we could be happy living together—working together—on my income. Now I hope you know that will be true."

The rector looked at her dumbly for a moment. Then his expression changed and he laughed suddenly, "But that won't be a problem at all now, will it?" Then, when he saw the confusion on her face, he added, "Surely I mentioned it?"

"What?" asked Claire, totally bemused.

"That I am the ninth earl," said Mr. Bennett, laughing. "You will not have to support me after all, my darling, though it is kind of you to offer. I cannot believe I hadn't mentioned it to you."

"You never gave the slightest hint that you were your cousin's heir," said Claire with some surprise.

"Perhaps I didn't," he admitted, "but, you see, I never really felt that I was. It had been my cousin's ondest wish to cut me out of the inheritance, and I never doubted of his succeeding. His first wife, bless her soul, failed many times to bear him a live heir. I think that with each failure he hated me more—and her, too, I'm afraid. His new wife is young and strong, so I'm told, and my cousin was certainly not too old to father children, so I never expected to succeed him. With all the grievances I had against him, it was better not to think of it.

"But she did not conceive—there cannot be any doubt of it now, I suppose, for his wife herself informed me in this letter that I am the new earl. We shall dower her handsomely; John cannot possibly have run through the entire estate."

Claire could still not believe her good fortune. To have Christopher for her own would have been enough, but she would have feared an uneasiness between them because of his lack of wealth. Now it seemed that everything was to be perfect. A thought suddenly gave her pause. She asked soberly, "What about your work here, and the Church?"

Far from the concern she expected, Christopher's face lit up with excitement.

"Don't you see?" he asked. "Now I will be able to do much more than I ever could have done through the Church. I will take my seat in the Lords and take them all on if I have to. It will be wonderful! And I will not neglect Garby parish," he assured her. "I will be very careful in my selection of a curate to make sure that what I have accomplished here is not undone. And I will check on him when I come to see my beloved in-laws."

Claire became caught up in his enthusiasm. They sat making plans, oblivious of the time, until Christopher recalled them to the present.

"You know what the greatest agony was for me?" he asked. "It was to see you with that fool Babcock and think that one day I might have to perform your wedding. I suppose I was all wrong."

Claire looked at him loftily. "I will have you know that I received a very pretty proposal of marriage from Lord Babcock only this morning," she said. "At least, I think that was what it was," she admitted, and she told him about the morning's events and the years of embarrassment that had led up to them.

Christopher laughed with the assurance of the victory. "Let's hope he consoles himself quickly with your cousin Lydia, if you are right about that being where his interest lies. I cannot believe anyone would prefer her to you," he said, "but perhaps I am old-fashioned."

"But he already has!" Claire exclaimed happily. "Isn't it marvellous for Lydia? We may not find it so," she said reasonably when she saw the doubt in his face, "but for her it is a glorious match. And he must love her very much to rush over there a scant half-hour after proposing to me. I know, because Uncle Bobby—"

Claire shrieked in midsentence. She struggled to get up.

"Steady!" said Christopher. "Where are you going in such a rush?"

"We must go!" Claire said urgently. "You must stop them! That's what I came here to tell you and I had completely forgotten about it. It's Uncle Bobby

He's done something terribly wrong. Oh, do let go!" she said, laughing, but serious.

Still, Christopher refused to relinquish his hold on her. He merely laughed and told her not to worry. "If this has anything to do with Tucker and the Derby, I have already taken care of it," he said.

"But how could you?" she asked in confusion. "I just found out myself, and Bobby wouldn't have told you. Surely he did not confess it to you!" she said in shocked tones.

Christopher smiled. "You ought to know by now that that is not your uncle's way. I am not sure that I approve of the confessional, but in Robert Willoughby's case it might not be a bad idea." He then told her about his encounter with Tucker. "I suspect that Tucker may not be coming back here, though. Something tells me that his character is too far damaged to change despite this reprieve. I have been keeping the money for a few days just to let your uncle get anxious. I thought it might do him some good to worry. Teach him a lesson."

"I would not be too optimistic about that," Claire said ruefully. "I have to conclude that my uncle is perfectly amoral."

Christopher laughed with such total delight that Claire felt compelled to ask what was so funny.

"I should have been more careful about whom I fell in love with," he said. "It occurs to me that I am about to inherit Robert Willoughby as an uncle. Do you think he will benefit from our future talks together, or do you think he will try to milk me of my fortune?"

Claire smiled and shrugged, looking at Christopher with love in her eyes.

"Babcock is an utter fool!" said the rector, pulling Miss Oliver close and kissing her again. "We will just let him deal with Uncle Bobby."

PAMELA BROWNING

...is fireworks on the green at the Fourth of July and prayers said around the Thanksgiving table. It is the dream of freedom realized in thousands of small towns across this great nation.

But mostly, the Heartland is its people. People who care about and help one another. People who cherish traditional values and give to their children the greatest gift, the gift of love.

American Romance presents HEARTLAND, an emotional trilogy about people whose memories, hopes and dreams are bound up in the acres they farm.

HEARTLAND...the story of America.

Don't miss these heartfelt stories: American Romance #237 SIMPLE GIFTS (March), #241 FLY AWAY (April), and #245 HARVEST HOME (May).

HRT-1

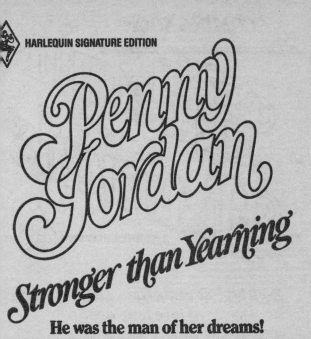